GOLD CITY GIRL

JO ANNE WOLD

GOLD CITY GIRL

Illustrations by
George Armstrong

F
Wo

Cop. 1

ALBERT WHITMAN & Company · Chicago

To my Mother—for all the faithful years.

ISBN 0-8075-2986-9; L.C. Catalog Card 77-165825
Text copyright © 1972 by Jo Anne Wold
Illustrations copyright © 1972 by Albert Whitman & Company
Published simultaneously in Canada by
George J. McLeod, Limited, Toronto

Contents

THE
TERRITORY OF
ALASKA
IN 1912

Yukon

St. Michael

B E R I N G

S E A

1 Off to the Summit

Kelly Hansen was almost out of the kitchen door when Ma called her back. A split second later on this April afternoon and she would have been gone.

What now? Kelly groaned inwardly as she stepped into the house. She had her heart set on going to the ridge summit to dig crocus. All day Ma had found one thing after the other for her to do.

"Why don't you ask someone to go with you?" Ma said as she tied an apron around her waist in that quick, brisk way she had of getting things done. "It's such a long way for you to go alone."

"Oh, do I have to?" Kelly asked, the tone of her voice matching the disappointment on her face.

"No, you don't have to," Ma answered, moving about the kitchen getting flour and pans out in preparation for bread baking. "I just thought you might like the company. Sometimes I think you should have more friends your own age."

"But there aren't any girls my age in Gold City," Kelly said, drawn into the argument unwillingly. Why didn't Ma just let her go and be done with it?

"Besides, I don't need any more friends. I have Harry Mudge and the bachelors at Walnut Creek and Flapjack Charlie."

"The miners are not your age," Ma reminded her.

"I know, but I like them better than—" Kelly had almost said, better than the Bramstead girls in Fairbanks, but she caught herself just in time. Ma thought Evelyn and Lucy Bramstead were perfect little ladies. "—Better than a lot of people I know," Kelly finished lamely.

Ma smiled indulgently. "Just go," she said, waving Kelly out the door with a flour-dusted hand. "But be back in time for dinner."

"I will," Kelly said, slamming the door before the words were out of her mouth.

Kelly wasn't her real name. It was the nickname her brother Tim had given her when he couldn't manage Katherine Eleanor. And Kelly somehow fitted her independence.

Free at last, Kelly sighed to herself. She splashed headlong through the puddle outside the back door. It didn't matter about the water. Her shoe pacs would keep her feet dry.

One day the ice on the wooden sidewalks is frozen as hard as iron. The next day it is a pool of water at your feet. That is how fast spring comes in Alaska.

With a great suddenness the season comes forward, spreading irresistibly across the valley, melting, thawing, loosening, letting go.

Kelly had seen so many Aprils like this. First in midmonth the ice cracks in the creek bed, then the water begins to show like a long black snake in the narrow trough made by the crack.

The honeycombed heaps of snow, no longer white, sag and sink under the sun's constant glare. The icicles on the cabin roofs drip faster and faster and fall to th ground with a wet clunk. On the air is the smell c_ damp earth, tangled weeds, and wet wood.

High, high on the hills bordering Gold City the fragile wild crocus lifts its fuzzy purple head above the rocks, braves the frigid air, and blooms. Spring has come.

For two years now, Kelly had planned to climb the summit near Gold City to dig crocus. There was a special place in the front yard where she wanted to transplant them. But somehow she had never gotten around to it. This year Kelly felt a great urge to get the job done. She didn't know why—it was just one of those things she *had* to do.

Kelly went to the summit alone because she liked it best that way. It meant she didn't have to talk if she didn't want to. If she felt like shouting or singing she could do that, too, and she wouldn't have to answer to anyone.

When Kelly reached the top of the summit, she sat on the upturned pail and looked down on the way she had come. Far below like a silver needle ran Crooked Creek, stitching together the zigzag collection of log cabins and buildings to make them a fairly respectable looking town in this year of 1912.

Even from this height, Kelly could pick out Pa's store with the big plate glass window gleaming in the sunlight. Right next door was their cabin, smoke curling out of the chimney, a sure sign that Ma was still busy in the kitchen. The other cabins, the one-room schoolhouse, the Red Dog Saloon, and the mining company camp were easy to spot among the leafless birch and aspen trees up and down the creek.

The first settlers had come to this part of the country when gold was discovered ten years ago. Now the big boom was over, but there was still plenty of gold in the ground. The miners just had to dig deeper and work harder to get it out.

It sometimes disappointed Kelly that her pa was not a gold seeker.

"I just don't have the gold fever like some people," Pa often said. "All I want is a chance to make a better life for my family. There's money enough to be made selling goods and services to the miners."

Pa dabbled in everything. Besides running the general merchandise store, he was agent for the

Northern National Bank, ran his own freighting business, and was postmaster to boot. The store was the headquarters for all of Pa's enterprises. When it came election time, the store was the polling place, and Pa was the election judge.

There was just one thing Pa hadn't counted on in Alaska. Doing business up here was not like running the little neighborhood grocery store in an Oregon town.

Up here Pa had to order enough merchandise in the spring to last all year. The goods were shipped almost three thousand miles by way of the Pacific Ocean and the Bering Sea, and then by a smaller vessel up the Yukon, Tanana, and Chena rivers to Fairbanks.

The cargo was then transferred to the narrow gauge railroad for a twenty-mile trip to the Gold City siding. At the siding, Pa loaded his wagons for the five-mile trip over the mud-clogged trail to the store.

By then all Pa's money was tied up in stock. The miners were honest people, but they charged food all winter, hoping to pay after the sluicing of the gold in the spring. Some years there wasn't enough gold. Then the bills didn't get paid.

This meant Pa had to borrow money from the bank to buy more stock. Every year it was like that. One year a warehouse fire ruined part of his stock.

"A vicious circle," Pa would say. "I just can't get ahead."

"You have to limit the amount people charge," Ma tried to tell him.

"I can't let anybody go hungry," he would reply.

"The least you could do is send out bills when people don't pay anything month after month."

"My customers know what they owe me," Pa would answer.

Kelly could remember hearing that same argument year after year.

The aunts in Oregon had begged Ma not to go to Alaska. "It's a hard country," they had said, concern stamped on their faces. "Uncle Horace lost all his money in Nome. Don't go."

Kelly remembered what her ma had said then. "I'll follow my husband wherever he goes."

And follow she did, with Kelly and nine-year-old Tim. When the family reached the port of Valdez, gateway to Alaska, deep drifts of wet snow lay on the ground. Jagged snowcovered mountains rose above the boomtown with its canvas tents, log cabins, wooden sidewalks, and harbor full of boats.

From Valdez, it was four hundred miles to the Hansens' destination: Fairbanks. The snowpacked trail to the gold rush town led a zigzag, up-and-down course over windswept mountains, deep valleys, and frozen creeks and rivers, deep in snow. The Hansens, bundled in fur robes to their eyelashes, made the trip in a horsedrawn sleigh. It took seven days of jogging over icy ruts between snowbanks five feet high to reach Fairbanks, deep in the interior of the Alaskan Territory. To six-year-old Kelly, the swishing of the sleigh runners sounded like her aunts whispering, "Don't go. Don't go."

Tim, Kelly's big brother, was good at remembering the strange-sounding names of the lodges along the trail. "There was Camp Comfort, and Eureka, Siana, Ptarmigan Drop, Tiekel, Tazlina, Gulkana, Gakona, Gillespie—" He would go on and on if Kelly didn't stop him.

At the lodges, dinner was waiting, usually moose meat roast with canned potatoes and sourdough bread served up family style at long tables covered with red-checkered oilcloth.

"I'll never eat moose again," Ma said after the fifth night of the same fare.

It was on that trip that Kelly and Tim learned to drink tea, gallons of it, piping hot, to warm them after twelve hours of traveling. They would fall into bed with their clothes on, only to be awakened at five the next morning to start all over again.

Kelly remembered the endlessly white trail, the faraway mountain ranges that caught the last rays of the fleeting golden sun, and dimly lit lodges with very cold water for washing.

Kelly thought that more than half of her life had passed since then. The aunts should see me now, she decided, thirteen years old, and looking more like a boy than a girl. She glanced down at her heavy breeches bagging over the tops of her shoe pacs. A dark plaid shirt buttoned under her chin matched the navy knit cap pulled over her ears. The aunts wouldn't like what they saw, Kelly knew that for sure. But she didn't care, not one bit.

The tingling cold summit wind dashed against her cheeks. Kelly was glad she was dressed for the weather. She knew how to protect herself against the harsh, unpredictable Alaskan climate. She knew how to survive in this land. Hadn't Tim taught her how to hunt rabbits, how to catch fish, how to run a dog team, how to start a campfire? She felt a contentment deep inside knowing she could take care of herself. There wasn't anything she couldn't do.

Is there a better place in all the world than this? Kelly wondered. Her eyes took in the narrow valley below, shimmering with glossy red-tipped willows and greening spruce trees.

The pale turquoise sky was full of light and would stay that way until past nine o'clock that night. Already there were eighteen hours of sunlight a day, a joyous time after the dark winter just past, when the stingy sun hovered on the horizon for only a few hours in the late morning.

That's why I feel so good, Kelly decided. It's the sun, the sun, the sun—and summer is coming.

"Oh, let me always be this happy," Kelly said out loud, jumping up and stretching her hands to the sky. She picked up the shovel and started digging, placing the crocus plants carefully in the bucket.

2
Unwelcome Surprise

Kelly's arms ached. Strong as she was, the bucket filled with crocus plants was too heavy. Ma was right as usual. Kelly had to stop several times going down the steep grade. Thank goodness it's always faster going home, she thought.

"Don't get too many," Ma had warned her when she left the house. "The bucket will be too heavy to carry."

When she reached the bank of Crooked Creek, Kelly was tempted to dump some of the flowers to lighten the load. But they would die, and that didn't seem right, so on she trudged.

It's my own fault for taking so many, she reminded herself as she shifted the load from one arm to the other.

Underfoot, the ground was spongy-damp from the spring runoff. In some places black pools of water stretched across the ragged path. Kelly waded through the shallow puddles, her boots making a sucking noise in the mud.

In the sheltered, shady woods the snow still held fast against the white birch trunks. By next week that snow will be all melted, Kelly thought, walking faster on familiar ground. Where the trail led upwards to the drier areas exposed to the sun, shoots of green could be seen among last year's tangled brown grasses.

The fine, clean smell of spruce shavings reminded Kelly that she was nearing Harry Mudge's sawmill. She was tempted to stop and visit with him. They always had lots to talk about together. Harry made her feel special. He treats me like a grown-up, that's what it is, Kelly had decided. It was hard to pass Harry's cabin without turning in, but Kelly made herself do it.

"I have to get the crocus planted before dinner," she said out loud to no one in particular.

She could have stopped to rest at any of the cabins along the way. Kelly knew all the families and the bachelors who built their homes on the mining claims along the banks of the creek.

Here at Crane Gulch, Jalmar Thorgaard had built his snug three-room log cabin chinked with moss. He had installed a front window, the biggest one on the creek, with crisscross panels at the top.

His wife, Bendte Thorgaard, was the best baker on the creek. Raised doughnuts and Swedish coffee cake were her specialty.

Maybe they are eating doughnuts right now, Kelly thought, and her feet dragged. No, she had to keep going. Besides, Rosemary and Isabel Thorgaard, both younger than Kelly, would ask her why she hadn't invited them to climb the summit.

Next along the creek came the Fessler cabin, where young Mike Fessler and his father lived alone since Mike's mother had died. Mike was a year older than Kelly. They had both attended the one-room schoolhouse in Gold City since she was in the first grade. Kelly hurried, hoping she wouldn't see him. Nowadays it was hard to talk to Mike. She felt bashful. It had never been like that before.

There was a stark, desolate look to the Fessler cabin, even though it was built of spruce logs like all the others on the creek. Some houses sparkle, almost as if they are smiling. The Fessler house seemed to pull away, shrouded in unhappiness.

The Fessler cabin is grieving, Kelly thought, and Mrs. Fessler has been gone two years now. Mike's dog, Bozo, ran close to Kelly's heels and barked, then sniffed and turned away. That was the only sign of life around the place.

Following in the creek path, Kelly passed the schoolhouse, Emmett Wilson's restaurant, Tom Saylor's cabin, and the Turnbarge place. Each log cabin had a pitched roof and silver smokestack. Next came Pa's store with the wooden sidewalk out front leading to their house next door. Across the creek were Pa's barns and the field where he planted oats. Not far down the path was the Red Dog Saloon, always under the watchful eye of Mrs. Turnbarge, who knew exactly who went in and what time they came out.

On downstream, farther than Kelly could walk this day, were the Exploration Company's mining camp, the three snug cabins of the Walnut Creek bachelors, the Bonovich family, and the small colony of Yugoslavs. Last along the line was Mrs. Lobaugh's pool hall.

Unpeeled spruce railings fenced the Hansen cabin where Kelly turned in. The gate gave its usual squeak. Eager to get the plants in the ground, Kelly forgot her aching muscles and started digging a flower bed near the front window. She carried water from the creek and then banked the bed with rocks.

"I don't know why you go to all that trouble," Tim said, coming into the yard, his boots clomping on the boardwalk. "You can get all the wildflowers you want out the back door."

"Not crocus," Kelly said, following him to the back porch where they scraped the mud off their boots.

"What's so special about crocus?" Tim wanted to know.

"They're first to bloom in the spring."

Tim shrugged. He still didn't understand. He

was too practical to think about things like that. About three years older than Kelly, he was more interested in earning money for college. He already had a summer job with the mining company, and school didn't close for another three weeks.

While other kids were thinking about getting a job, Tim was working. Kelly was proud of her brother. He was the smartest one in school. He had long outgrown anything Gold City school could offer.

Tim was changing so fast. It kind of scared Kelly, as if she were living with a stranger. These past months, Tim's body had lengthened and filled out. His voice was deep and mellow most of the time. One day he was a boy, the next day he was a man. It seemed to happen just like that. His hair, dark and curly like Pa's, grew long on the back of his neck. Ma threatened to tie ribbons on it.

Am I changing, too? Kelly wondered as she set the crocus plants into the ground. If she was, she couldn't tell. Heaven knows, she consulted the mirror often enough for proof. Her arms and legs were still spindly straight, as shapeless as the willows outside her bedroom window.

Tim had changed in other ways. He kept more to himself. Kelly couldn't quite put her finger on it, but Tim was aloof, not just from her, but from Ma and Pa, too. He didn't join in family things the way he used to do. If Ma insisted that he join them skating on the creek or pulling taffy in the kitchen after dinner, he would do it, but not in a free and willing way. That was the difference.

Often when Kelly saw Tim sitting alone just staring into space she would ask, "What are you thinking about?"

Usually he would mumble, "Oh, nothing much," and walk away.

But once he said, "I'm thinking about leaving this place. There is a big world away from Gold City, and I want to see all of it."

Leave this place? Kelly couldn't understand his feelings. Everything she loved was right here. She didn't think she could be happy in any other place. She belonged here.

Kelly didn't say these things to Tim—he would think she was childish. She didn't ever want to leave this creek town, and she didn't want Tim to leave either. She wanted everything to stay the same. She wanted her family to be together always, with Pa working every day at the store, and Ma cooking in the kitchen or sitting in the big chair and sewing by the light of the kerosene lamp.

Kelly wanted the seasons to come and go and nothing to change. There would be holidays for tree trimming, and birthdays for celebrating with double-decker chocolate cakes with pudding in the middle as only Ma could make them.

Let these things go on forever, Kelly thought as she took the last crocus plant from the bucket. Deep inside she knew that could never be. Things change, people change—sometimes slowly, sometimes suddenly. You never know how or when the changes will take place.

Where will I be next year at this time? That was a game Kelly liked to play. But no matter how she tried, she could never imagine herself being anywhere but right where she was.

Kelly and Tim went into the house. Ma was pulling a pan of shortcakes from the oven. The good baking smell filled the room. The heat from the big kitchen range steamed the cool window panes. When Kelly was younger, she used the panes as a writing slate, drawing pictures until the moisture was all gone.

Even if Ma wasn't my mother, Kelly thought, stepping into the room, I would still think she was beautiful. Evangeline Hansen had kept her slim bridelike figure while other women had gone to wide hips and bosoms. Her hair, still a deep chestnut brown flecked with red, was wound in braids on top of her head. Her skin held a rosy, healthy glow.

"What's for dinner?" Kelly asked, pouring hot water from the teakettle into the washbasin. "I'm starving!"

"Moose stew and blueberry shortcake," Mrs. Hansen replied.

"Umm, good," said Kelly.

"When you finish washing, Kelly, go out and get some blueberries from the cache. Pa will be home soon."

Kelly quickly dried her hands and grabbed a spoon and pan from the cupboard.

"Don't slam the door," Ma called after her.

"I won't," Kelly answered. The door slammed anyhow. It was always like that.

The root cellar, dug deep into an embankment, was at the far end of the backyard. A wooden door, lined with tarp, gave an eerie squeak as Kelly pushed it open.

She squinted her eyes to adjust to the inky blackness of the cache. As she groped along the dirt wall to find the candle holder, Kelly was afraid she would touch a spider or something worse—she wasn't sure what that might be.

She struck a match, inhaling the pleasant sulphur smell, and lit the candle. The feeble, wavering light enabled her to find her way past the gunnysacks of potatoes and the wooden keg of sauerkraut to the barrel of blueberries. Kelly remembered those berry-picking days of last summer as if they were photographs in her mind, full of intense sunlight with everyone smiling wide to show his purple teeth.

Kelly had to scrape the bottom of the barrel to get enough berries for dinner. The cycle of planting and harvesting and filling the root cellar was about to begin again. It gave Kelly a sense of security knowing the family was capable of doing it.

When Kelly returned to the house, Pa was there and everyone was sitting at the table. The conversa-

tion stopped abruptly when Kelly opened the door, as if they had been talking about her.

"What took you so long?" Tim said to cover the awkward silence.

"I was only gone a few minutes," she said defensively. Kelly sensed there was something wrong. She slipped into her chair, and Pa gave the blessing.

While the food was hot the family filled their plates, eating quickly until their first hunger was satisfied. Ma set an abundant table. All the miners hinted for an invitation to the Hansens. "With Ma cooking, it helps to own a grocery store," Pa said.

When it came time for seconds, the Hansens ate more slowly, taking time to tell of the day's activities.

Tim was saying, "Pa, I figure if I work all summer at the mine, I'll be able to save about two hundred dollars. When I graduate from high school, I should have enough money for college."

Tim wanted to make his job at the mine sound important because he wasn't going to work at the store this year. Ever since Tim was ten, he had worked for Pa. He didn't like the grocery business. Besides, there wasn't much money in it for him. Tim wanted to be an engineer. Working in the mine would be good experience, he told Pa.

"Just don't count on all that money before you get it," Pa answered. "Things don't always turn out the way you want them to."

Tim shot a quick glance at Kelly. She made a face at him. Why was he acting so odd? Ma was looking at Pa as if she expected him to say more.

"A man came into the store today," Pa said finally. He leaned back in his chair and pulled on his suspenders. "He offered me a pretty good deal."

Kelly was instantly alert. That's what they were talking about when I came in, she thought.

"The Commercial Trading Company in Fairbanks wants to buy the store. A new mining company is moving into Crooked Creek to put up a dredge. The trading company has a contract to supply all the goods they need."

"Oh, no," Kelly said. "You aren't going to sell out, are you, Pa?"

"It's something to think about, Muffin," he said. Pa always called her that when he was trying to make things easier for her. "This past year hasn't been a good one at the store."

Kelly nodded. She knew all about that—bills and payments, bills and payments.

"Maybe someone else could run the store better," Pa said sadly. It wasn't easy for him to admit defeat.

"But if another mining company comes in," Kelly said, "then you could make more money."

"The only trouble is," Pa said, "I don't have the money to stock all the things the company needs."

"But what would you do, Pa?" Kelly asked. She

couldn't imagine what it would be like in Gold City without Pa in the store. It wouldn't be the same at all.

"Well—" Pa said hesitantly.

The bad part is coming, Kelly thought.

"The trading company offered me a job at their store in Fairbanks."

"Leave Gold City?" Kelly shouted. "You don't mean leave Gold City?" Tears were streaming down her face. "We can't, we just can't."

Tim started forking food into his mouth as if nothing was wrong. But Kelly knew what he was thinking. If they moved into Fairbanks, he could go to high school there. He wanted to leave Gold City. How could he be such a traitor?

"We haven't decided anything yet," Ma said. "Pa just told us about the offer. We have to think about what is best for all of us."

The unbidden tears continued to roll. "I know that, Ma," Kelly said, "but it would be so hard to leave our good house and all our friends." She wiped her tears, feeling foolish because everyone was looking at her.

"It would be a big change for all of us," Pa said. "There is no hurry. We have until August to think about it. We would keep our house here and maybe come back in the summer to work the ground."

His words were soothing, but Kelly sensed a new series of events had been triggered, and she was helpless to do anything about them.

Pa changed the subject, and dinner dragged to an end. Kelly helped Ma clean the kitchen. Neither spoke of what was on both their minds.

Leave Gold City, Kelly thought. She dried the dishes, not really aware of what her hands were doing. Leave Gold City—never wade in the creek water again; never play cards with Harry Mudge on a winter night while the Yukon stove sends red sparks up the chimney; never see Mike come skiing down the slope near the schoolhouse, his bug light blinking in the morning darkness. She would miss Mike. The thought came to her so strongly she had to admit it.

Kelly folded the damp dish towel and left the house to walk along the creek. To her there was something comforting about the undisturbed flow of water moving on toward some unknown destination, never resisting the steady surge forward.

Kelly sat on a tree stump tossing wood chips into the clear creek water, watching them float downstream, around the bend and out of sight. There was a distinct coolness in the April air since the sun had dropped behind the summit, sending up an apricot blaze against the darkening sky. Usually the joyful sound of Crooked Creek rolling over the rocks lifted Kelly's spirits, but not tonight.

What to do? Kelly thought. There must be a way we can stay here. If only Pa could get enough money to stay one more year. That's all I ask. Just one more year. I can't leave now. I'm not ready.

3
Nothing Stands Still

Lining the windowsills of the Hansen cabin were tin cans washed clean, filled with dirt, and sprouting sturdy green plants. In late March Mrs. Hansen started the seeds indoors so they would be ready for planting this last day of May.

Without a head start the cabbages and celery, string beans and beets, would not reach maturity during the short subarctic summer.

In the backyard garden plot the Hansens would plant a good-sized patch of potatoes, set out onion bulbs, and string lines for pea vines.

The wooden slat fence surrounding the yard was not entirely successful in keeping out the greedy rabbits that came in the night or the baby moose on teeter-totter legs. Kelly didn't mind sharing the vegetables with the animals. It was Ma who got upset when all the cabbages down the line were sampled.

Kelly made her fifth trip carrying plants to the garden where the black soil lay freshly turned in the hot sun. Kelly remembered the years the family worked to clear the land—felling trees, burning brush, digging tree stumps and carting rocks to the creek. Pa hauled load after load of topsoil from the peat bog down the road. The hard times were behind them. The ground was just the way they wanted it.

It was a perfect day for planting with just enough breeze to keep the mosquitoes away, but that did not improve Kelly's disposition. Why are we even planting a garden? she thought. We probably won't be here to harvest anyhow.

The threat of leaving Gold City hurt like a tight knot in her chest. No one talked about selling the store and leaving, but the possibility was there, as obvious as a wart on a nose. But everyone chose to ignore it.

Well, I can't ignore it, Kelly thought as she carried a bucket of water from the creek. I can't pretend everything is the same when it isn't.

The summer had lost its savor. All the things Kelly loved about the season—the unplanned days, the freedom to roam the valley and the hills— seemed empty and meaningless. Last week when school was dismissed, Kelly didn't join the kids for the annual picnic with Miss Elliott. Instead she walked home alone dragging her feet in the dust, feeling sorry for herself and wanting to cry, but the tears wouldn't come.

I can't even talk to Ma about it, Kelly thought, glancing across the yard where Ma was stringing lines to mark the garden rows. Kelly sensed there was a barrier between them, as if Ma didn't want to talk about the possible change. It wasn't the right time. Sometimes you have to let things be, Kelly told herself.

"Do the cabbages first," Ma called.

"All right," Kelly answered, getting down on her knees. The task ahead seemed endless and the row of cabbages a mile long. Over and over Kelly had to dig a small hole, pour in water, shake the plant from the can without disturbing the roots, pat the dirt around the plant, and water again.

Better get busy, she thought, or I'll be here all day. She worked silently while the sun blazed hotter and hotter in the cloudless sky.

During the last few days the leaves had started to uncurl, sticky and shiny, from the budded branches of the birch and aspen. A fat robin redbreast called invitingly from the rustling foliage. Despite the heat and the light breeze, a few hungry mosquitoes buzzed around Kelly's head. From time to time she stopped to swat the bugs and scratch the red lumps on her neck and wrists.

At midday Kelly and Ma stopped for lunch, carrying a pitcher of lemonade and a plate of sandwiches to a shady place beside the house.

"I don't think we will ever get rid of the dandelions," Mrs. Hansen said, scanning the side yard. Ma's efforts at a lawn resulted in a few patches of "real grass" among an abundant crop of wild grass, chickweed, and foxtails, dotted with scads of yellow dandelions.

"Harry said all those flowers should be put to use in dandelion wine," Kelly remarked. But we probably won't get to make it now, she added silently to herself.

"When you finish the next row," Ma was saying, "why don't you take a box of plants to Mrs. Bonovich? Her family didn't have much of a garden last year."

"Do I have to help her plant them?" Kelly asked.

"No," Ma answered. "I'm sure Mrs. Bonovich has her own ideas about that."

But her ideas are always wrong, Kelly thought, remembering last year how Mrs. Bonovich had started her garden on the fifteenth of May because "that's how we do in old country." All the seeds froze in the ground. By the time Mrs. Bonovich admitted failure, it was too late to plant anything except leaf lettuce and carrots, and a spindly crop they were. The family was destined to a winter diet of canned vegetables. Kelly didn't envy them.

It was the Bonovich children Kelly felt sorry for, young Hilda and Einar. Mrs. Bonovich had so frightened ten-year-old Hilda and six-year-old Einar about the dangers of living in this wild country that they were afraid to leave the yard.

Sometimes Kelly persuaded Hilda to walk with her along the creek or visit Flapjack Charlie at the mine. Hilda always predicted they would fall into the water or come upon a bear. They never did, but Hilda's fears held fast.

At school Kelly helped Hilda with her lessons. It wasn't easy because Hilda understood little English. "I like you talk slow," Hilda said to Kelly. "I can learn more English."

Heaps of white clouds moved across the sky, casting huge shadowy patterns on the slopes of the hills, as Kelly started for the Bonovich cabin. She took the wagon road where the walking was easier than along the creek path.

Her shoes made a scratch, scratching noise on the loose rocks. She walked leisurely, in no hurry to return home to more planting.

Mrs. Bonovich will probably find something wrong with the vegetables, Kelly thought. "Not good like in old country," Kelly could just hear her say it. I won't let her bother me this time. I won't, I won't, Kelly promised herself, as she made her way past the familiar landmarks along the road—the fallen tree where the wild bees stored honey and the pond where water lilies bloomed in late summer.

Up ahead, smoke curled out of the cookhouse chimney at the Exploration Company Mine. Flapjack Charlie is making pies for dinner, Kelly thought. She would stop at the mine on her way back to walk home with Tim.

In the air lingered the smell of burning wood and leaves. The bachelors of Walnut Creek, a tributary of Crooked Creek, were still cleaning their yards. In the springtime, in the summertime, and in the fall, the ground around their trim cabins was swept as spic-and-span as a polished plate. The windows of their cabins gleamed. The firewood stacked nearby was as straight and precise as words on a printed page.

Kelly waved at Mr. Heinsmith who was raking a few twigs in a small burning pile. "You raked your yard last week," she called.

"Ja!" Mr. Heinsmith answered, looking up from his work. "I don't know where the mess comes from."

"It's the cleanest yard in Gold City," Kelly said.

"That is true," he nodded, and there was a lively twinkle in his blue eyes. He pulled off his wide-brimmed hat revealing a crown of curly gray hair. No matter what the weather or the season, Mr. Heinsmith wore a gray wool shirt and gray wool trousers held up by wide suspenders. A gold nugget watch chain was draped across his chest. Mr. Heinsmith was never without his watch chain.

The three bachelors—Mr. Heinsmith, Curly Mawler, and Gus Anderson, "The Great Dane," they called him because he came from Denmark—worked the same mining ground, but lived in separate cabins.

All the children of Gold City liked Mr. Heinsmith. He would spend the whole afternoon telling them stories, teaching them card games, and delighting them with magic tricks.

One summer, as Kelly would never forget, Mr. Heinsmith invited the children to come see his "apple tree."

An apple tree—that is not possible in Alaska, everyone said. Apple trees can't grow this far north. But there in Mr. Heinsmith's yard were apples hanging from a tree. One by one, and hour after hour, Mr. Heinsmith had tied apples to the limbs of a small birch tree just for the pleasure he knew it would give the children.

Of the three miners, Curly Mawler had the most fascinating cabin. It had all the usual things like a bunk bed built against the wall, a small wood-burning stove with a shiny tin stovepipe going right up through the ceiling, wooden crates nailed to the wall for cupboards, and a table and a few mismatched chairs for entertaining visitors.

It was the walls of Curly's cabin that were so unusual. From floor to ceiling they were papered with covers from the *Saturday Evening Post* magazine. You could look this way and that for an hour or more and never see them all. Every time Kelly visited Curly she discovered a new picture.

Kelly rested on a tree stump while she talked to Mr. Heinsmith. "Where are Curly and Gus?" she asked.

"They are working in the mine and waiting for water. We need a good rain."

Kelly nodded. The miners said the same thing every year. The pay dirt, the gold-bearing gravel from the underground mines, was now piled in mounds near the sluice boxes. Before the precious

metal could be extracted, water was needed to wash away the dirt and gravel.

The pay dirt was shoveled into elevated troughs, called sluice boxes. Water running in the sluice boxes carried the dirt to a pile on the ground. Gold, being heavier than dirt, would sink to the bottom of the sluice box. There the nuggets and flakes of gold were caught and held in the riffles, or wooden slats, until the miner was ready to scoop out his treasure.

"I think it will rain tomorrow," Kelly predicted as she stood up to leave. "The gardens need rain, too."

"That's good, that's good," Mr. Heinsmith chuckled.

Kelly walked on. The road narrowed before it reached the Bonovich cabin. There wasn't much coming and going this far downstream. Hilda and Einar saw Kelly and held the gate open for her.

"You come! You come!" Hilda said excitely, jumping up and down, her dark braids bobbing on her shoulders. Her dress, made of the same checked gingham as Kelly's, was tied at the waist with an embroidered sash of some silky material. She held a fringed shawl around her shoulders. Because Hilda dressed differently and talked with an accent, the girls at school laughed at her.

"Hallo, hallo, hallo," Einar chanted. His dark eyes fringed with black lashes beamed happily whenever company came.

"Hello," Kelly said, grabbing his small hand in hers. "Have you planted your garden yet?" she asked, following Hilda to the cabin door.

"No. We have no garden this year. Nothing grows in this country."

"That isn't true," Kelly protested. "We had vegetables all winter from our garden."

"You have better dirt," Hilda said. She was like her mother, never admitting there might be something wrong with the way they did things.

No arguing with her or any of the Bonoviches today, Kelly reminded herself. Mrs. Bonovich met them at the door. She was a tall, lean woman with olive skin and heavy black eyebrows that moved expressively when she talked. "What you bring?" the woman asked, her dark eyes roving curiously over the plants in Kelly's bucket.

"Cabbage and celery," Kelly answered. "They should be planted today."

"How you do that?" Mrs. Bonovich asked.

"I'll show Hilda how to plant them if you want me to," Kelly offered, even though she hadn't planned to stay that long.

"Good, good," Mrs. Bonovich said abruptly and closed the door, leaving the two girls and Einar standing on the porch.

The garden soil was packed hard and scattered with small rocks and a tough network of weeds and roots. With Hilda and Kelly digging with shovels and Einar following behind with a hoe, they soon readied a small space. Kelly showed Hilda how to put the plants in the ground.

"It's the same every time," Kelly said. "Be sure you leave a space between each plant so it can grow."

"You really think the vegetables will grow?" Hilda asked warily. "Nothing ever has."

"They will this time," Kelly promised.

It was late afternoon by the time Kelly left the Bonovich cabin. Tim has probably left for home, Kelly thought, hurrying along the road. At the mine she ran up the steps to the cookhouse and pressed her face against the screen.

"Flapjack Charlie," she called, "did you see Tim leave yet?"

"Just a few minutes ago," he said, coming to the door, his wooden leg making a thumping noise on the floor. "If you run, you can catch up with him."

"Thanks," Kelly called over her shoulder. She ran as fast as she could, her dark hair streaming behind her. In the place where the road straightened for half a mile, Kelly spotted Tim.

"Tim," she called, "wait for me."

He was sitting on a grassy hummock by the side of the road when Kelly reached him. She was breathing hard and holding her side.

"Oh, I ran too fast," she said, and tumbled down beside her brother. They rested in silence, letting the warm sun burn against their cheeks.

40

Swallows nesting nearby swooped by them to nip mud from the roadside ditch.

"The iris are blooming," Kelly said suddenly, sitting up straighter and shading her eyes. "Look, Tim," she said, nudging her brother and pointing to the grassy green plant with a purple flower.

"I saw those last week," Tim said.

"Why didn't you tell me?"

"I didn't think it was important," Tim answered. That was Tim—he would never change. "Come on, let's go," he said. "I want to ask Ma if I can ride over to Stampede Creek. They have a dredge operating over there."

"When did that start up?" Kelly asked, walking quickly to keep up with her long-legged brother.

"Last week."

"Is it the same kind of dredge the mining company is going to have in Gold City?" Kelly asked.

"Yeah," Tim replied.

"Can I go with you?" Kelly asked.

Tim never got mad when Kelly went places with him. They were as companionable as friends. Kelly never fought with her brother the way some brothers and sisters fight. The only time Kelly and Tim argued was when they carried water from the creek. Tim would slip a wooden rod through the bucket handle. As they walked Tim let the bucket slide until Kelly was carrying most of the weight. Even after Kelly caught on to the trick, he still tried to get away with it every now and then.

"Tim," Kelly said hesitantly, "I've been thinking about Pa selling the store and all. I figured if I worked in the store this summer, Pa could work our mining property and pay off the bank."

"Pa already tried working that property and it cost him more than he made," Tim reminded her. "That ground isn't worth working full time. Besides, Pa doesn't like mining. You know that."

"I know," Kelly said, "but if he just got enough gold to keep the store . . ."

"It won't work, Kelly. You don't know enough about the store to run it alone," her brother said. "You might as well forget it."

Kelly hadn't expected a lot of encouragement from Tim, but she didn't think he would dismiss the idea so completely. I'm not going to forget it, she thought. I'll talk to Pa. He will listen to me.

When they reached home, Ma gave them permission to ride over to Stampede Creek. "Be careful," Mrs. Hansen called from the backyard as Tim helped Kelly up on the horse.

"We will," they said in unison, leaving the yard at a dignified trot.

After they passed the store, the saloon, and the schoolhouse, Tim urged the horse to a faster pace. The trees and bushes were a green blur as they flashed along the trail. Before Kelly knew it, they had passed Harry's cabin. She tightened her arms around Tim's waist. She didn't like to ride so fast, but she didn't say anything.

Kelly was relieved when they started to climb the summit. The horse had to go slower. Here above the timberline only a few shrunken spruce trees, a drab green color, grew among the rocks and lichen.

In a few weeks the wild flowers would bloom, great colorful sweeps of yellow-centered daisies, purple Arctic lupine, masses of buttercups, and the yellow tundra rose. The sides of the hills would blaze with the pink alpine shooting star. In the quiet places close to the earth, the creamy-white rock jasmine would open its beauty to the sky.

The trail skirted the summit ridge for more than a mile before making a crooked course down the slope to Stampede Creek. Above the sound of the horse's hooves Kelly heard another sound. It was a high-pitched screeching and creaking noise unlike anything she had ever heard before.

"What is that noise?" Kelly yelled in Tim's ear.

"It's the dredge," he shouted back.

Stampede Creek was like the other creek towns that sprang up wherever gold was discovered. The general store, the saloons, the restaurant, and sometimes a bakery, were just log cabins with false storefronts. There was a wooden sidewalk and a muddy road, wide enough to let two wagons pass, that led to the mining claims.

It didn't take Kelly long to discover there were changes at Stampede Creek. Along the road, stands of trees had been cut, leaving a crop of yellow stumps. A newly-blazed road branched off the main trail to the dredging company camp. There was more travel than usual, loaded wagons and men on horseback traveling purposefully to and from the mine. All the time that howling, piercing noise filled the air.

Kelly's heart beat faster. Is this what will happen when the dredge comes to Gold City? she wondered.

Tim followed the road until he came to the campsite. There among the trees a cookshack and bunkhouse had been hastily built. Kelly could see a man still working to finish the bunkhouse. He was nailing down sheets of tin on the roof. Sawdust and leftover lumber littered the yard.

In a large pond of water beyond the bunkhouse Kelly saw the dredge. It looked like an oddly shaped ocean-going vessel with a long trough at the stern and a floating bucketline at the front. The buckets were mounted on a squealing, screeching conveyor belt. Each bucket in turn scooped up gravel from the bottom of the pond. The dredgemaster in the control house operated the machine to keep the buckets moving continuously.

The buckets automatically dumped their gravel into a bin inside the dredge. From there the gravel flowed to a large revolving screen used to sift out the gold ore from the coarser dredgings. The excess rock and debris, called oversize, then moved on a conveyor belt through the huge trough to the tailing piles on the banks of the pond.

The undersize, the finer gravel which contained the gold, sifted into a riffled sluice box where mercury was used to attract the gold. Every two weeks the dredge was shut down to remove the mineral.

Tim guided the horse to a small rise above the dredge. "Look at that," he said, marveling at the size of the machine. "The dredge can do the work of hundreds of men. Think how long it would take to dig all that gravel by hand and sluice it."

Kelly wasn't impressed. She hated the dredge at first sight. It threatened all the things she loved most —the quiet beauty of the mining town and the hard-working miners who took gold from the ground with a pick and shovel.

"I'm going down to see if they'll let me on the dredge," Tim said. "Do you want to come?"

"No," Kelly said, sliding off the horse. "You go ahead. I'll wait here."

She watched Tim ride down the slope. Everything is changing too fast, Kelly thought. She walked away from the dredge to a wooded area untouched by the movement of men and machines. Last year's leaves and spruce needles rustled under her boots. A quick brown squirrel hustling up a tree, chattering to the birds as he went, made Kelly smile. The sunlight fell in jagged patches on the ground.

This is the way I want things to be, Kelly thought, sitting on a fallen tree. How long can it last?

The high-pitched squeal of the dredge beyond seemed to answer, "Not very long."

4
Kelly Keeps Store

There was the good morning smell of bacon frying in the skillet and the sound of Ma's spoon hitting against the bowl as she mixed a batch of sourdough hot cakes. On the back of the range the coffee perked, filling the house with its strong aroma.

"Time to get up, Kelly," Ma called.

The light coming through the cotton curtains touched the wooden dresser and the washstand and traveled up the walls. The rough-planed logs had been covered with cheesecloth and then with wallpaper in a small floral design. The ceiling was wavy with layers of cheesecloth and paper. Canvas stretched tight across the floor was painted a deep red to match the flowers on the wall.

"Aren't you up yet?" Ma asked, bustling into the room with a pitcher of hot water for washing.

"Right away," Kelly said, rubbing her eyes and forcing herself to sit up. She wished she could jump out of bed and get dressed fast the way Ma did every morning.

Then Kelly remembered what day it was. Pa had agreed to let her work in the store while he went to Fairbanks. Better get up and show Pa I'm really serious about helping him, she decided. Kelly had hinted to Pa that she could run the store all summer while he worked in the mine. Pa wasn't too taken by that idea. "I'll think about it," was all he had said.

Kelly moved quickly from the warmth of her bed to the curtained closet. She chose her navy blue dress with the sailor collar. That will look business-like, she decided. After washing in the china bowl on the washstand, Kelly slipped into her clothes. She brushed her hair, fastening it in back with a white ribbon.

She flipped the blankets over the bed and fluffed the pillow. There were lumps in the middle, and if Ma saw it, she would probably tell Kelly to make the bed over again. But it was worth the chance. What was summer vacation for if you couldn't leave your bed sloppy just one morning?

"Where's Tim?" Kelly asked as she got busy setting the table.

"Getting water," Ma answered, stacking hot cakes on a huge platter. "Put the plates in the oven," she reminded Kelly. Ma insisted on warming the plates for hot cakes.

Pa came banging in the back door, carrying an armload of kindling. "Make way," he said, heading for the woodbox behind the stove. "That should take care of you until I get back."

He brushed himself off, then gave Kelly's long hair a yank as he passed her. "How's my business partner this morning?" he asked.

"Fine, Pa," Kelly said, giving him a big smile. Pa was always in a good mood when he went to Fairbanks. In a way, Kelly wished she were going.

Pa made those trips to town so special. They packed a lunch to eat on the train, but in the evening before returning home they stopped at the Model Cafe to order steak and onions and fried potatoes. Sitting in the high-back booth, being served by a waiter in a black suit and long white apron, and listening to Pa's friends talking until the very last minute before the train pulled out of the depot, was Kelly's idea of a perfect evening.

Fairbanks is fine as long as you don't have to live there, Kelly reminded herself.

Tim came staggering in under the weight of two five-gallon buckets of water.

"You shouldn't carry such a heavy load," Ma scolded him when he joined the family at the table.

"I didn't want to make two trips," he explained. "Besides, the buckets don't seem so heavy after shoveling all that dirt at the mine."

Tim worked underground in the mine tunnels where the pay dirt was hacked out of the ground with picks and shovels. It was Tim's job to load the pay dirt into trolley cars and roll the cars along the narrow tracks to the main shaft. There the ore was emptied into buckets carried to the surface by steam-operated hoists.

"Have they started to sluice yet?" Pa asked, forking five hot cakes on his plate and adding plenty of butter and blueberry syrup.

"A little," Tim answered. "They pumped some water from Crooked Creek to wash a couple of loads. We need a heavy rain before we can really get rolling."

Kelly passed the plate of bacon. "I wish it would rain every day so we wouldn't have to water the garden by hand." She had lost count of the trips she made from the creek with the watering can.

"Just be glad the creek is right outside the back door," Tim said, "and not a mile through the woods."

Ma got the coffeepot from the stove. "Some summers are too dry, others are too wet. There never seems to be a happy medium," she said.

The Hansens finished breakfast with little conversation, each one thinking ahead to the jobs that awaited.

"I'll do the dishes," Ma said to Kelly. "You go over to the store. Don't forget to ring the bell if you need anything."

"I won't forget," Kelly replied, letting the screen door bang behind her. Pa had strung a cord fastened to a bell in the kitchen between the store and the house. Whenever Pa wanted to signal the house, he pulled the cord. I won't need to use that, Kelly thought, as she walked briskly across the yard.

She used the key to open the back door. Kelly liked the first whiff of the store with all the smells mingling together—the coffee beans waiting to be ground, the spices in marked jars, the starchy newness of material stacked in bolts, the leather bridles hanging from the rafters.

The store was so crowded. Pa stacked the shelves and tables to hazardous heights to make room for all the merchandise. The rows of canned goods were lined four deep, the barrels of crackers and dried beans and boxes of dried apricots, prunes,

and apples were pushed tight together side by side against the counter.

Pa made room on one side of the store for clothing and household goods. On the shelves were china plates, tin water dippers, silverware, washbasins and pitchers, bedrolls and pillows, rubber boots and overalls, along with mining tools—picks, shovels, gold pans, rope, kerosene lamps, and candles.

Kelly walked up and down the aisles trying to remember where everything was located. I don't see how people can find anything, she thought.

Kelly started to straighten the pile of work gloves and woolen stockings, but by the time she was finished, she had also rearranged the table of pots and pans and hunting knives.

She was working in the kitchen supply section when she heard a voice behind her say, "What are you doing?"

Kelly whirled around and in her excitement she knocked over a stack of dishes. Some of the plates crashed to the floor, scattering in a hundred pieces.

"Oh, Mike!" she cried. "Look what you made me do." Kelly was down on her knees. "I broke all these plates." She sat back on her heels, wanting to cry, but holding back the tears because Mike was there.

"I didn't mean to scare you," he said, helping her pick up the pieces, "but the front door is locked so I came around back."

Kelly jumped up. "The door is locked. Oh, no!"

She hurried to the front of the store. Mike was right. She had forgotten to unlock the door. A great business partner I turned out to be, she thought.

She gathered a broom and dustpan to finish cleaning up the broken china. When she had that job out of the way, she asked Mike in her most businesslike voice, "Did you want to buy something?"

"I came to get some stuff for Harry," he answered. "I'm working for him this summer."

"You are," she said excitedly, forgetting her problems. "What are you doing?"

"Loading wood and hauling it to the mine. I started last week."

Already there was a change in Mike. His face was tanned, and his blond hair, with that lock that always fell across his forehead, was bleached from the sun. There was a confident set to his wide shoulders, a greater assurance to that long-legged stride of his.

"Let me see your list," Kelly said, "and I'll get your things for you."

She quickly assembled the order. It came to three dollars even. She was glad of that—making change was still hard for her to figure.

"Is your father working his mine?" Kelly asked, not wanting Mike to leave.

"He took in a partner, and they sank the shaft too deep and it filled with water. I guess they're going to start a new hole. I don't know for sure. I don't see him very often. Pa said I could work for Harry until he needs me at home."

Kelly nodded. She knew it wasn't easy for Mike since his ma died. Every night his pa was seen at the Red Dog Saloon. Mike had to shift for himself. It must be lonely for him, Kelly thought. I'm glad he can be with Harry. She wanted to tell him that her family might sell the store and move to Fairbanks, but she couldn't make herself say the words. It would seem too real then.

They both heard the sound of footsteps on the wooden sidewalk. Mrs. Turnbarge's heavy silhouette passed the window. Oh, why does she have to come now? Kelly thought.

"Guess I'd better be going," Mike said abruptly. "I'll see you."

Before Kelly could think of anything to say, the boy had picked up his packages and ducked out the back door.

"Helloooo, Kelly," Mrs. Turnbarge said in her singsong voice. "How are you today?"

"Fine," Kelly replied, forcing herself to smile. There was something about Mrs. Turnbarge's brisk, know-it-all manner that rubbed Kelly the wrong way.

"Was that the Fessler boy that just left here?" Mrs. Turnbarge asked.

"Yes," Kelly answered, thinking that there Mrs. Turnbarge goes again, poking her nose in other people's business.

"My, he is getting tall and good looking, too, just like his father. I hope he doesn't have all his father's ways." She smiled knowingly at Kelly. Mrs. Turnbarge's house was across the creek from the saloon. She kept track of all the customers.

Kelly was finding it hard to be nice to the woman. "Is there something I can get for you?" she asked, wishing the woman would get what she wanted and leave.

"Are you alone in the store?" Mrs. Turnbarge wanted to know. "I don't see your pa."

"He went to Fairbanks," Kelly answered. "I'm helping out today."

"Your pa sure knows how to keep the whole family working," Mrs. Turnbarge said with that quick little laugh of hers. She had a way of cutting people down. If the kids worked, then the parents were taking advantage of them. If they didn't work, then the kids were lazy. There was no way to win with Mrs. Turnbarge.

"We got in our order of scented glycerine soap," Kelly said, attempting to get Mrs. Turnbarge on to the business at hand.

"Oh, did you?" Mrs. Turnbarge said. "I bought some in Fairbanks."

It's just like her, Kelly thought. She never tries to give Pa extra business. She only buys things here when she can't get to town. Then she charges everything.

Kelly remembered overhearing Ma talk about

the big bill the Turnbarges had run up. Mrs. Turnbarge was better at running other people's affairs than her own. Her husband could never make enough money to keep up with her spending.

"Do you have any silk embroidery thread?" the woman asked, walking over to the sewing counter.

"Yes," Kelly said, following her. She handed Mrs. Turnbarge the box of thread.

"Oh, you don't have the right shade of green. I guess I'll order it from the catalog," she said.

Kelly put the box back on the shelf. "Is there anything else?"

"I don't suppose you have any of those silver buttons," Mrs. Turnbarge said, stirring her finger around the button box. "No, you certainly don't. I didn't really expect that you would."

Kelly clenched her fists. "We don't have room to stock all those specialty things," she said, trying to keep her voice under control.

"I never can find anything I need in here," Mrs. Turnbarge said. She had a way of getting in the last word. "I'll just get a few groceries then."

Kelly weighed the dried apricots and raisins and got the canned milk and tin of butter Mrs. Turnbarge requested.

"Add that to the bill," the woman said, gathering up her purchases.

The way she said it, in such a superior tone, as if she was doing the Hansens a favor by coming in the store, triggered Kelly's temper. It's people like

Mrs. Turnbarge who keep Pa in debt all the time, Kelly thought. In a moment of anger, Kelly held Mrs. Turnbarge responsible for the threat of moving to Fairbanks.

"About the bill," Kelly said, her voice quavering. She could hardly believe she was saying the words, but now that they were out, she had to go on. "We would appreciate a payment."

Mrs. Turnbarge's cheeks went fiery red. "Who are *you* to discuss such a thing with *me*?" she exclaimed. "You mind your own business, young lady!"

With a sharp bang of the front door she was gone.

I shouldn't have said that, Kelly thought, slumping against the counter. I shouldn't have said that. She tried to justify her actions, but no matter how right she thought she was, Kelly knew Pa would not like what she had done.

Kelly worked hard to keep from thinking about the encounter with Mrs. Turnbarge. She swept the floor and rearranged the wooden armchairs around the potbellied stove where miners gathered so often in the wintertime to talk about the gold they hoped to find. As the men talked, darkness would settle against the snowbanks, and the lowering temperature outside would make the log building pop and crack.

With each passing winter hour it was harder for the men to leave the warmth of the fireside for their own cold cabins. Many times Pa was an hour late for dinner because his customers, buying only a plug of tobacco or a tin of pickled herring during the long afternoon, forgot to go home.

Pa is just too good-hearted, Kelly decided as she straightened the stack of magazines on the table. Maybe he shouldn't be in business for himself. Kelly paused a minute in her work. Do I really mean that? she asked herself. Would Pa be better off working for someone else? Why does life have to be so complicated? Why can't things stay the same?

It was late evening, and still Pa had not returned home. The sky was full of light. The moon, a pale opal disc, was lost among the white clouds in the blue sky. It didn't get dark anymore at all. Sometimes it was past midnight before people remembered to go to bed.

Kelly and Tim were on the front porch playing checkers when they heard the clip-clopping of Dolly's and Bravo's hooves on the road.

"It's Pa!" Kelly yelled, jumping up and running to meet him.

Pa hitched the horses to the fence post. He put his arm around Kelly's shoulder as they walked to the house. "All your old boyfriends at the Model Cafe asked about you."

Kelly smiled. Pa sure knew how to make her feel good.

Ma heated the coffee and they all had a piece of pie while they discussed the events of the day.

When the conversation got around to Kelly, Pa asked, "How did things go in the store?"

"Oh, pretty good," Kelly said, but she couldn't meet Pa's eyes. "I did break a couple of plates," she confessed. But that wasn't the thing she knew she should tell him.

"Don't worry about that," Pa said. "I can always order more."

Good-hearted Pa, there he goes again, Kelly thought. "I rearranged some of the merchandise," she added.

"I bet I won't be able to find a thing tomorrow," Pa laughed.

Kelly knew she should tell Pa about Mrs. Turnbarge, but she couldn't. I'll tell him tomorrow, she promised herself. She couldn't stand it when Pa was upset with her. He never got mad. It was more that he was disappointed in her, and that hurt worse than a spanking.

Kelly went to bed while Tim helped Pa unload the wagon. She lit the small tin of special powder by her bedside to keep the mosquitoes away.

I'll tell Pa about Mrs. Turnbarge tomorrow, Kelly promised herself. It hadn't been a very successful day, she decided. Saving the store was not going to be an easy task at all.

She lay for a moment with her eyes wide open watching the smoke curl upwards from the little tin to the ceiling. As soon as she closed her eyes, she was asleep.

5
Fishing with Harry

With each day that passed, Kelly found it harder and harder to tell Pa about Mrs. Turnbarge. Had she, Kelly, really dared to hint the overdue Turnbarge bill should be paid? Maybe it wasn't so important after all, but she really knew better.

In the back of her mind was the nagging feeling that Mrs. Turnbarge would tell Pa about Kelly's behavior. That would make the situation worse, much worse. She should tell Pa herself.

But if I don't think about it, she reasoned, maybe it will go away. This was an easy solution to the problem.

Pa let her work in the store two days a week, which didn't seem like very much at first. But now it was getting to be a bore, Kelly decided. Nothing was happening in Gold City, unless you happened to see Charley Carter working on the new community hall. There'd be a dance there when it was finished, but that seemed a lifetime away to Kelly.

Kelly sat on a stool, resting her elbows on the counter, waiting for the bell over the door to ring. There had been no customers for the past hour. She could hear Pa working in the back room. She thought that he could always find something to do. She supposed she should, too.

She sighed deeply and didn't move from her spot. At the store it was the same old thing every day. Sweep the floor, carry out the wastepaper, put cans on the shelf, take cans off the shelf, wrap packages, make change (she was getting better at that), then start the whole routine over again.

Kelly felt trapped. When she was working, she wanted so much to be outdoors where the birds were calling in the trees and the sun was spanking brightly on the creek water ready for wading and fishing.

If she did take time off from the store, she felt guilty about not helping Pa. What to do? More than once Kelly wondered if it really mattered. Would Pa sell out in spite of what she did?

"Kind of quiet today, isn't it?" Pa said, coming up behind her.

"It sure is," Kelly agreed, sitting up straighter.

"I'll tell you what I'm going to do," Pa said, the way he always did when he was getting ready to spring something he had been thinking about for a long time. "I'm going to let you go down to Harry's and see how the grayling are biting in the creek. If you bring home a mess of fish for dinner, we'll call that a good day's work. How's that for a bargain?"

Kelly slipped quickly off the stool. "Oh, Pa!" she cried, hugging him. "That's a great idea. Can I go now? Right now?"

Pa nodded. Kelly danced around him and then flew out the door.

"Don't forget your fishing pole," Pa called.

"I'll use one of Harry's," she called back over her shoulder. She didn't want to waste any time getting there.

Harry was down on his knees, weeding in the garden, when Kelly reached his place. The sun was shining fiercely on his bald head.

"Why aren't you wearing your hat?" Kelly asked, leaning against the garden fence. She liked to fuss over Harry, and he liked to let her.

"I can't find it," he answered, crawling along the row of sprouting plants and plucking out the healthy crop of weeds that had sprung up among the cabbages. "It must be in my cabin some place. You don't think my eyesight is failing, do you?"

She shook her head until her pigtails hit her in the face. "No, not at all," she said emphatically. Harry could still spot a moose among the foliage before anyone else could.

"I see you have already eaten some leaf lettuce

and green onions," Kelly said as she surveyed the garden patch.

"I have to have my green stuff after that long winter," Harry said.

The radishes, round and red, would be ready next. The first ones were best plucked from the soil, wiped on the seat of the pants, and dipped in salt. Harry always left a salt shaker under a tin can in the garden to make carrot and radish eating all the better.

"Do you want me to help you weed?" Kelly asked, hoping against hope that he would say no. She wanted to go fishing so badly.

"I'm almost finished with this row," Harry said. "Then I thought I'd take my best girl fishing."

Kelly clapped her hands. "Oh, do you mean it?" she said. "I was hoping that's what you would say."

"I'll get the poles and some bait from the shed," he said, getting to his feet. His steps were energetic, like a boy's.

"I'll look for your hat," Kelly offered, keeping in step beside him. "Do you want me to pack some food?"

"You must have guessed I baked cinnamon rolls this morning."

Kelly made her way to Harry's cabin which was surrounded by a thick growth of fast-growing lamb's-quarters. Some people called the plants weeds, but Harry welcomed them. It took forever and ever to pick enough of the small leaves to get a serving. "It's worth it," Harry said every year, "it's better than spinach."

Kelly skirted the patch of wild strawberry plants that sent runners out halfway across the yard. The strawberry blossoms were waxy white against the pale green leaves. The no-bigger-than-a-thumb-nail berries would be forming soon. It took hours and hours to get a pail of those, too.

The minute Kelly stepped inside the cabin she spotted Harry's hat hanging on a peg over his bed. He must have looked right at it, she thought, smiling to herself. The cinnamon rolls, freshly turned on a plate, were cooling on the table. It didn't take Kelly long to wrap several rolls in paper and head out the door.

With fishing poles bobbing over their shoulders, the cinnamon rolls tucked under Kelly's arm, and a bottle of citronella in Harry's pocket to drive off the mosquitoes, they set off for that spot along Crooked Creek where the grayling bite the best.

They hiked upstream along the trail a quarter of a mile without seeing a single person. Even with the calling of the birds and the noises of the squirrels up and down the tree trunks, there was a kind of silence all around them. Now in June, the trees had lost that delicate green of spring. The leaves had taken on a deeper color and grew thicker and broader with every passing day.

When the two of them reached the spot where Crooked Creek made a crook and was shaded by a heavy growth of alder bushes, Harry paced back and forth along the creek bank. He said he did this to get the feeling that the fish were here and they would bite. It was a ritual with him that Kelly respected. They never went home empty-handed.

Wild lupine and a scattering of bluebells grew in clumps along the grassy bank. There Harry spread old papers on the ground so they could sit and fish.

"Some people say you aren't really fishing unless you are standing in the creek," Harry said as he settled himself on the bank. "But, by golly, if I can do a job sitting down, that's the way I'll do it."

Dangling her feet over the bank, Kelly agreed, "Me, too. This is the life."

She tossed her line in the water and grabbed a cinnamon roll. Leaning back on her elbows, she looked up at Harry with eyes squinted against the sun. Her skin was shiny with citronella to keep the mosquitoes away, and she liked its fragrance.

"Do you really think there's any grayling down there?" she asked.

"Sure, there's grayling down there," Harry answered. "Just watch. I'll show you."

He made a great production of it, too. First he clapped his hat on the side of his head, adjusting it several times to get just the right angle. "Sun gets hot on an old man's head," he explained.

66

Kelly grinned. He always said that when he was fixing his hat. She could depend on it sure as Crooked Creek flowed downhill. And he could say "old" if he wanted to, but he didn't seem old to her. He was just Harry—bald head, bristly gray whiskers, blue eyes, and careworn hands—just Harry, not young, not old.

He took a few seconds to untangle his fishing line. Once he was satisfied with that he plunged the hook into a dead fly without batting an eye. With a quick jerk of his arm he cast the line into the water. It fell with barely a splash next to Kelly's. Carefully he got to his feet. There was a pleased expression on his face. "A-haa!" he said. "I got one."

"Already?" Kelly cried. "How do you do it? Your line is right next to mine and I didn't even get a nibble."

"Experience, my girl, experience," Harry said smugly.

He pulled a ten-inch grayling from the water. The fish flopped, wiggled, gasped, and finally gave up.

"We're on our way to dinner," Harry smiled.

In a few minutes he had two more fish flopping on the creek bank. He cleaned the fish with his knife, slitting them down the sides, cutting off their heads, and scraping the scales. Long ago he had taught Kelly to do the same thing. A good fisherman never takes home uncleaned fish. That was his rule, and if you wanted to go fishing with Harry, that's the way it was done. The cleaned grayling were wrapped in grass and put inside a bag.

"I wish I knew all the things you know," Kelly said, letting her rod bob up and down in her hands as she stared at the water.

"What is it you want to know, my girl?" Harry asked. He had figured all along that she had something on her mind.

"It's just that everything is changing so fast," Kelly said, knowing she wasn't explaining very well what she felt. "I don't know what to do," she ended in a whisper, afraid that tears would be next. She didn't take her eyes off the water.

"What is changing?" Harry asked, not certain of what she meant.

"People change. The things we do change," Kelly mumbled. Finally looking up at him, she said, "Oh, Harry, don't you know? Pa might sell the store and we might move to Fairbanks."

Harry didn't speak for a minute. At first Kelly thought he was going to say, "Is that all that's bothering you?" But he didn't. Not Harry.

He did say, "Some people might like that kind of change."

"Tim would," Kelly said scornfully, "but not me. I belong in Gold City with you—and everybody."

She lifted her hands helplessly and then let them fall limp in her lap. If Harry didn't understand what she was talking about, then she didn't know what she would do.

"When we are happy," Harry said slowly, pushing his hat back on his head, "we don't want people or things to change. But changes come, and we can't stop them."

I thought Harry would be so understanding, Kelly thought to herself, and here he is talking in circles like everyone else.

"But, Harry," Kelly said, swatting a mosquito away from her face, "I've lived in Gold City almost all my life. Living in Fairbanks scares me. I wouldn't know how to act or what to be."

She remembered how Ma always said she should have friends her own age. But instead she had the miners and Flapjack Charlie. When other girls were playing with dolls, Kelly was playing cards with Harry or Tim. When other girls were worrying about a party dress, Kelly was learning to run a dog team or skin a rabbit.

"I just don't belong in the city," she said.

"You know," Harry said in that kind of drawl he used when he was getting ready to say something important, "when you live in one place for a long time, and you know everybody, you kind of get set in your ways and forget to grow."

Kelly wanted to say out loud, "You aren't making much sense," but she held her tongue. I'm not set in my ways, am I? she asked herself.

"Sometimes," Harry went on, "when we get too satisfied with a place, it's time to move on. It means we need a challenge to bring out the best in us. Not everybody gets a challenge or faces up to it when it comes along."

There was a look on Harry's face that Kelly had never seen before, a sadness that went back to something Harry had tried to forget. "I had a challenge once," he said, "but I turned my back on it. I don't regret the kind of life I've led, but I sometimes wonder if I didn't take the easy way out."

Kelly had never seen this side of Harry before, a troubled and perplexed side. She was sorry she had started a conversation that put a damper on their beautiful day.

"It's not that you want to stay in Gold City," Harry said, "but that you are afraid to go to Fairbanks."

Kelly lifted her head quickly to look at Harry, her blue eyes searching his. "I never thought of it that way," she said, catching her breath. "I'll have to think about it."

Harry touched her hand. "Don't think about it too much," he said. "There are fish to be caught." The upward turn of his lips made Kelly smile, too.

"I know," she responded, "and you are already ahead of me."

A breeze ruffled the pointed tops of the trees and swished across the creek bank, carrying the spicy fragrance of tamarack needles and other green and growing things. Kelly wrinkled her nose and sniffed appreciatively.

"Ummm, do you smell that?" she asked.

Harry clapped his hand to his chest and inhaled deeply. "Let's bottle it and make a million," he laughed.

Kelly felt a slight jerk on the end of her line. There it was again, only stronger. "I think I have something!" she said excitedly.

Kelly pulled in the line, making it taut, according to the patient instructions Harry had been giving her for years. He sat without moving, smiling his approval.

"That-a girl, that-a girl," he said.

Kelly stood up and dug her heels into the sand. She needed all her strength to pull in the fish. "I got him!" she cried. "I got him!" The fish flopped at her feet. "Look how big it is!" she marveled. "Isn't it a beauty?" Her grayling was a good three inches longer than Harry's.

Harry scratched his head. "How do you do it?"

"Experience, my man, experience," she laughed.

"You are getting too smart for me," Harry said, pulling in his line. "I think it's time we headed home."

Kelly cleaned her fish while Harry packed up the gear. The walk back to the cabin seemed shorter than the walk from the cabin to the creek. The trip home always seemed shorter. Kelly could never figure out why. The distance covered was the same.

Harry tried to explain. "It's your anticipation to get someplace that makes the trip there seem longer, and your reluctance to go home that makes it seem shorter."

Harry was full of all kinds of explanations like that. It made Kelly think that he knew more than anybody else in the whole world.

She would think about the other things he had said this day, turning them over in her mind and examining them as carefully as she would examine a rock that might contain gold.

It's not that you want to stay in Gold City, but that you are afraid to go to Fairbanks, Harry had said.

Is that it? Kelly wondered. Is that what's wrong with me?

6
Deep Trouble

Ever since Kelly had awakened, her thoughts had been occupied with one thing, and one thing only—the dance tonight at the new community hall.

The day had dawned fair and warm with only thin wisps of clouds like patches against a blue sky.

Kelly was sitting on a grassy place in the side yard, drying her hair in the sun. The dark strands were soft from the rainwater she had used. Her hair glinted red wherever the sunlight touched it just so.

In the distance, Kelly heard the sound of Charley Carter's hammering. He was finishing work on the new community hall where the dance would be held. All the families from Gold City would be there, plus many from Stampede Creek, Sara City, and as far away as Chatanika.

The youngest of the children would be carried in wearing their nightclothes. As the evening progressed, the babies and toddlers would be bedded down in the side room and lulled to sleep by the sweet strains of Duncan Wiseman's violin and Joe Kaplenski's accordian.

Before the community hall was built, the dances had been held in the Red Dog Saloon. Mrs. Turnbarge had complained, "It just isn't fitting to take children into a place like that." She had been the prime worker in getting the hall built.

The fact that the new hall was without a piano was no problem. Ma's piano, her prize possession and the only piano between Gold City and Fairbanks, would be carried by seven husky and willing young miners from the Hansen cabin to the community hall. Ma would follow them, her skirt trailing a bit on the dusty road, giving instructions along the way.

"I hope they are just as willing to carry the piano back to our house in the morning," she'd fret.

During the evening, the tables would be spread with the potluck supper. The women tried to outdo each other by frying the crispest chicken, mixing the tangiest potato salad, or making the most savory baked beans. And the desserts—why, the tables would fairly sigh beneath the load of pumpkin pies, spice cakes, custard cups, molasses bars, and raisin cookies.

Mrs. Thorgaard would bring enough sugared doughnuts to feed an army, and not a single one would be left to take home. Not that she cared. It was considered a compliment to have the plates left empty.

Kelly's thoughts about the dance were interrupted when Ma, her figure a shadowy outline inside the screened porch, called, "Kelly, Pa rang the bell. Run over and see what he wants."

"All right," Kelly answered.

Pa was opening cartons of canned vegetables in the back room when Kelly entered the store. A dark blue apron covered his white shirt and dark trousers. Pa's face was clean-shaven except for a full black moustache that curled up like a smile. His black hair, kinky-curly, was brushed back crisply from his forehead. Everybody said Kelly had his eyes, deep-set and of the bluest sea blue. Kelly was glad of that.

"I just got a message from Reverend Bramstead," Pa said, talking and working at the same time. "He and the two girls are at the train siding waiting for a ride. They are coming to spend the night."

"Oh," Kelly said, not too enthusiastically. She was thinking that they *would* have to come the night of the dance. That could spoil everything.

"Walt is taking the wagon to pick them up. Why don't you ride along?"

Kelly felt like saying, "Do I have to?" But she knew the answer. She had to.

The Reverend Mr. Bramstead and his wife had been friends of the Hansen family ever since the Hansens had arrived in Alaska. The first winter, the Hansens had stayed at the Bramstead home, right next door to the log Episcopal church where Mr.

Bramstead preached.

There was no church in Gold City. When the ministers came from Fairbanks, they held services in the schoolhouse. Sometimes the socalled Sunday services were on a Thursday or Friday night. It all depended upon when the preachers could come. Kelly liked it that way. You never knew what the next day would bring. It was more exciting than having every day planned out.

"When is Walt leaving?"

"Right away."

"My hair is a little wet," Kelly said, offering the only excuse she had. It was worth a try.

Pa paused in his work and gave her his Don't-pull-that-trick-on-me look. He didn't have to say a word.

When Walt pulled up in front of the house, Kelly was waiting on the porch.

"The mosquitoes are bad on the trail today," Walt called from the wagon.

"I'll get my hat," Kelly said, disappearing into the house and returning with the wide-brimmed fawn-colored felt hat, tied around with mosquito netting. She didn't like to wear the thing—it was hot as well as being ugly. While it did stop the mosquitoes from biting her face and neck, it couldn't stop the constant buzzing which was almost as bad as the biting.

"That hat would do you more good if you wore it instead of carried it," Walt said to Kelly.

"I know," Kelly said agreeably, climbing up beside him on the wagon seat.

"Maybe the bugs don't like your flavor," Walt said, chuckling at his own joke. He slapped the reins over the horses' rumps and they started up the road.

"Oh, they like me all right," Kelly said. "I just don't like to wear the hat."

Walt hunched forward, keeping his eyes on the road to avoid hitting the deepest holes and ruts. He had a kind face and laugh lines wrinkled near his eyes and mouth, even though he didn't laugh much anymore.

Walt had come to Gold City one rainy night three years ago, built a cabin in the woods, and hired out to do odd jobs for the store-keepers—hauling wood, sweeping floors, dumping garbage. He didn't want to be tied down to any one thing. He preferred working when he felt like it. Somehow, he had the knack of being around when people needed him, like today.

"My little girl would be your age now," Walt said, letting the horses take a leisurely gait.

"What was her name?" Kelly asked. She had heard some of this story from Pa. Before Walt came north, his wife and daughter had been killed in a train crash. He rarely talked about them.

"Her name was Ramona. She was a smart one. She had hair like spun gold."

The way he said it made Kelly catch her breath. He missed them so, you could hear the sorrow in his voice. "I don't know what I would do without Ma or Pa or Tim," Kelly said. "I don't think I could stand it." The thought of losing anyone in her family disturbed her. Life would never be the same. It would be as if some part of me was gone and I would never be a whole person again.

"The wound heals over," Walt said, but there was a sadness in his eyes that Kelly could see.

"I want everything to stay just the way it is," Kelly said. She fingered the veil of her hat. So far the mosquitoes hadn't bothered her at all. The sun hit her squarely in the face, but she didn't care.

"That isn't possible for any living thing," Walt answered. "Try to stop a tree from growing, or a bird from leaving its nest. It isn't natural for things to stay the same."

Kelly had to think about that. Wasn't it natural for her family to stay in Gold City? She couldn't see anything wrong in that.

She didn't dwell long on such subjects. The day was too beautiful. From where she was sitting Kelly could see flashes of the creek through the trees. To her the sound of the water gurgling, bubbling, tumbling over the rocks and around the bends was the sweetest music in the world.

"Walt," Kelly said, interrupting his private thoughts, for he could go a mile or more without saying a single word, "don't you think Gold City is the best place in the world to be?"

"It's about as good as the next place, I reckon.

There isn't much difference that I can see. One mining town is about like the other."

"Oh, Walt," Kelly said impatiently, gesturing with her hands. "Look how beautiful it is here, and the people are so friendly. All the miners and everybody."

"You find that wherever you go, if you look for it," was Walt's answer.

Kelly folded her hands in her lap. "I suppose you are right," she had to agree.

Even before they reached the railroad siding, Kelly could see the Bramsteads waiting on the platform. The two girls were sitting back to back on the suitcase, their full skirts covering their high-button shoes. Their father was pacing back and forth beside them.

"There's Kelly," Lucy called, jumping up and waving her arms.

" Hello," Kelly called. "I hope we didn't keep you waiting too long. We didn't know you were coming."

Walt halted the horse beside the platform. Dust rose in yellow clouds from the wheels.

"We sent a letter. Didn't you get it?" Lucy asked.

Her pale skin was sprinkled with a fine peppering of freckles. Her greenish blue eyes were framed by gold-tipped lashes. A sunbonnet was tied over her yellow hair.

"No, we didn't get it," Kelly replied. "But you

know what the mail service is like."

"I hope we're not putting you people out," Mr. Bramstead said as he placed the big suitcase in the back of the wagon. His tall, bony frame was clothed in a black suit with a clerical collar. He looked unbearably hot.

"Oh, it's no trouble at all," Kelly answered him politely as her ma had taught her. "Wouldn't you like to ride up front, Reverend Bramstead? I'll ride in back with the girls. You know Walt, don't you?"

"Yes, of course." The minister settled himself on the seat while the girls arranged themselves in the wagon bed.

Evelyn carefully smoothed the folds of her lavender skirt. The material lent a violet hue to her eyes, tinting them like the center of a dark flower. Her glossy auburn hair curled below her shoulders. On her head she wore a straw bowler hat with a band of green at the crown.

Lucy and Evelyn look like pictures in a magazine, Kelly thought, taking in Lucy's flower-sprigged frock tied with a pink sash. Kelly hadn't bothered to change her faded blue gingham—it had seemed presentable enough when she left the house.

"We didn't think you were ever coming," Evelyn sighed, holding her hand to her cheek. "It was so hot in the sun. I hope I didn't burn my face. Did I? Does it look red?"

Kelly leaned forward. "No, Evelyn," she assured her. "It looks fine."

The railroad siding was at the top of the summit where the vegetation was sparse. Only scrubby spruce and dwarf birch trees grew here. The sun beat down with great intensity.

"And the mosquitoes," Lucy whined. "They are worse here than they are in town." She had red welts on her hands and arms to prove it.

"They don't bother me," Kelly said. She hoped she wasn't going to hear a lot of complaining from the girls. Evelyn and Lucy were always finding fault with Gold City.

"Why don't you let me wear your hat then?" Evelyn said, whipping off her own. Kelly handed her the mosquito net hat.

"That looks funny," Lucy giggled, pointing at her sister.

Whenever Kelly was with the Bramstead girls, it made her glad she had a brother instead of a sister. Evelyn and Lucy quarreled all the time, usually about little things that didn't amount to a row of peas. Evelyn was bossy and critical of her younger sister. Sometimes Kelly thought they didn't like each other at all. She dreaded the thought of going to the dance with them.

"What do you do all summer?" Evelyn asked.

"Oh, I go fishing or work at the store or visit the miners," Kelly answered. It didn't sound very exciting when she talked about it. But Kelly was convinced that no matter what she said, the Bramstead girls wouldn't like it.

"Is that all?" Evelyn said, making a face. "I hate to go fishing. Those awful worms and smelly fish."

Lucy giggled, forever echoing her sister's reactions.

When the wagon arrived at the Hansen house, Ma and Pa were waiting out front to greet the Bramsteads.

"Looks as if you girls plan to stay all summer," Pa said as he lifted the suitcase out of the wagon.

"Father is preaching at Stampede Creek and Sara City before we return home," Evelyn said in that prissy, precise voice she used for adults.

"All I need when I travel is a bag of beans and some sourdough starter," Pa laughed.

The Bramstead girls giggled.

"Oh, Pa," Kelly said, a trifle embarrassed. Men seemed to show off in front of Evelyn and Lucy. Kelly wondered how Tim would react to Evelyn now. Usually they were at dagger-points, Evelyn taunting him to pay attention to her and Tim refusing. Kelly had a feeling that would all be changed.

Ma and Mr. Bramstead led the way into the house with the others following.

"I wish Mrs. Bramstead could have come, too," Ma was saying.

"She doesn't like train rides," the minister said, his voice soft and low-pitched. Kelly wondered how he ever got up enough volume to preach a sermon.

He did though. On the church platform, Mr. Bramstead came alive. His eyes flashed a startling blue. His face became animated with the fervor of his convictions, and all the time his long hands gestured dramatically. Still waters run deep, Pa always said. There must be something to that, Kelly decided.

"I hope we aren't putting you out on such short notice," Mr. Bramstead added.

"Not at all. We look forward to company," Ma replied.

"Kelly said there is a dance tonight."

"Yes, there is. I hope you will join us."

"I think that would be fine," the girls' father replied.

Ma settled her guests comfortably at the big round table in the kitchen and served them sweet lemonade made with fresh-dipped creek water. A plate of cookies, the oatmeal kind with fat raisins and chopped nuts, was passed. A flood of afternoon sunlight poured in the south window framed with red-and-white checked curtains. Red geraniums flowered on the sills. It was truly the best room in the house—Kelly always thought that.

There was nothing in Ma's manner that indicated there was anything amiss. Outwardly she was her own serene, hospitable self. Kelly had no warning of the doom about to befall her.

"I would like to see you in your room, Kelly," Ma said. "Excuse us for a minute," she said to the visitors.

Kelly followed obediently, supposing Ma was going to suggest she let Evelyn and Lucy sleep in her bed and Kelly sleep on the floor. She was already prepared to do that.

"All right, young lady," Ma said, closing the door firmly behind her and facing Kelly head on. "What is this about Mrs. Turnbarge?"

There was a sick feeling in the pit of Kelly's stomach. Her throat was dry when she tried to swallow. "I-I was going to explain it all," Kelly said lamely, her eyes downcast. She twisted her hands together. This is the worst time for this to happen, Kelly thought. "I knew you and Pa would be mad," she ended on a mumbling note.

Ma was staring at her with those piercing dark eyes that could practically see what you were thinking.

"I'm sorry I did it, Ma. I'm really sorry."

"Pa and I were very upset when Mrs. Turnbarge came over today and told us about it."

I knew she would tell on me, I just knew it, Kelly thought, the big troublemaker.

"You know how Pa feels about asking people for money," Ma went on, her face stern. "You interfered in something that was none of your business."

"I know."

There was silence between them, punctuated by the ticking of the clock on Kelly's nightstand.

"It will be a while before Pa lets you work in

the store again. You cannot go around doing things just to suit your own purposes." Ma's voice was still angry.

Kelly started to defend herself, but then she held her tongue. It was true Mrs. Turnbarge criticized everything in the store. She was the worst customer they had, and she did owe money. But Kelly knew Ma was right, she had interfered in something that was not her business.

"I'm sorry," Kelly repeated. What else could she say? There was no need to make it a big family quarrel. Kelly cringed, thinking how she would feel if the Bramsteads got in on the whole thing.

Ma wasn't finished with her yet. "I'm very unhappy with you, Kelly. I just don't know what is getting into you these days."

Kelly didn't have any answer to that. I haven't changed, she thought. Everybody else has.

Ma turned to leave, then paused. "If the Bramstead girls weren't here, I would make you stay home from the dance." She went out the door, leaving Kelly standing alone.

Kelly wanted to slam the door her ma had left open, but she didn't. She threw herself on the bed and buried her head in the pillow.

The dance she had anticipated so eagerly was turning into a disaster. Now she had the Bramstead girls to thank for being able to attend. That was the worst cut of all.

7
Run, Kelly, Run!

"What's the matter, Katherine Eleanor Hansen?"
Harry Mudge asked, his voice reaching her over the
scrape of the violin and the wheeze of the accordian.
He called her by her full name when he wanted to
cheer her up. And here at the dance Kelly needed
cheering up, Harry observed.

Those blue eyes of his didn't miss much. Harry
knew Kelly, and knew her well. He had watched her
grow from a hesitant child into a confident girl. He
knew the many moods reflected in her face: stub-
bornness by the set of her jaw, gaiety by the flash of
her eyes, unhappiness by the pout of her lips.

"Oh, it's nothing," Kelly said, but she didn't
mean it.

She slipped into a chair beside Harry's. His
dependable loyalty gave her the reassurance she
needed.

The dance was proving the failure Kelly had expected after the episode with Mrs. Turnbarge had come to light. It had been bad enough before, when she'd had to welcome the Bramstead girls.

Joe Kaplenski was playing another polka on his accordian. Kelly could feel the beat of the music even though she was seated. The new dance hall, still smelling of fresh-cut lumber and sawdust, gave the miners and their partners plenty of room to dip and sway. The dance floor, hand-planed by Charley Carter, was waxed with the shavings from a hundred miner's candles.

Although it was past ten o'clock, sunlight poured through the small-paned windows lining the hall. The sun didn't know when to go to bed these June nights. Neither did the people.

As long as Duncan Wiseman could fiddle and Joe could play the accordion and Ma was at the piano, the dance would go on and on. Kelly groaned. She wished the whole thing were over now. She could go home and go to bed, and then Sunday would hurry by, and the Bramsteads would leave.

Evelyn and Lucy with fluttering eyelashes, coy smiles, and helpless giggles had captivated Tim as well as Mike. Kelly was disgusted with all of them. She refused to look across the room, where they were chasing each other around the chairs.

Harry patted her hand. "It isn't as bad as you think."

"Yes, it is," she said emphatically.

"When there are new faces in town it always causes a stir," Harry commented. "It won't last long."

Kelly wondered how Harry knew what she was thinking. She glanced at him. His skin was as pink as a child's, with hardly a wrinkle for his sixty years. There was not one speck of hair on his shiny head. And yet it was plain he remembered what it was like to be young.

"I'm not like other girls," Kelly said, leaning close to talk in his ear above the sound of the music. "I can't go around acting silly so some boy will follow me."

Harry chuckled deep in his throat. "You don't have to be like other girls," he said, filling his pipe as he spoke, his gnarled fingers moving slowly. "Just be yourself."

Kelly pulled her skirt so that just the tips of her black patent leather shoes showed. She had dressed carefully this evening. Her white dress with lace appliques on the bodice and sleeves was freshly starched. A pink satin ribbon caught up her hair in the back.

"It isn't always easy to be yourself," Kelly replied.

"It's easier than trying to be somebody else."

"I suppose you are right," Kelly agreed. "But no matter what I do, nothing turns out right this summer."

Ma was still mad at her. And all evening Kelly

had purposely avoided Mrs. Turnbarge. She didn't want to come face to face with her. She might have to apologize, and Kelly had no intention of doing that.

Pa wasn't really mad, but he wasn't happy with her, either. Then there was that Mike Fessler. He had hardly paid any attention to her all night. There he was, falling all over that flibbertigibbet Lucy Bramstead.

Kelly fumed. The more she thought about it, the madder she got. How would the Bramstead girls like it if she went into Fairbanks and took all their friends away? She could show them a thing or two! But she didn't even want to think about going to Fairbanks. The idea of moving there was already poisoning the whole summer.

I don't fit, Kelly thought unhappily. Kids my age are all dumb. I don't like the things they like. I'd rather be with Harry.

At that moment Harry said, "Let's dance. It's a good song."

The music was "Daisy, Daisy, Tell Me Your Answer True." Before the song was over, Kelly and Harry and the other dancers were singing.

"I feel better now," Kelly said, her eyes shining warmly.

"Go back to your friends and have a good time," Harry said.

Kelly approached the group of young people with some hesitation. Tim and Mike and the Bramstead girls had been joined by Rosemary and Isabel Thorgaard, their plump cheeks rosy pink with excitement, their eyes like lighted candles as they hung on every word the two city girls uttered.

"Hello there, Kelly," Lucy called in a voice that seemed overly friendly. "Where did you learn how to dance? I wish I could dance. Mother never lets us." She spoke breathlessly.

"I've been dancing since I was eight years old," Kelly answered. "Pa taught me."

"Do you just dance with old men?" Evelyn asked. The other girls giggled, holding their hands in front of their faces. Mike and Tim turned away.

I'd like to hit her, Kelly thought. That's what I'd like to do. She took a step forward, clenching her fists. But then Kelly restrained herself. She stepped back and said firmly, "Harry is not an old man. He is my best friend."

She walked away, leaving Evelyn without a word to say. In a small way, Kelly felt she had scored a victory. She wasn't sure how, but the feeling was there.

In the side room, Mrs. Collins was setting up the tables with food for the potluck supper. A big pot of coffee on the stove sent out a welcoming fragrance.

"Is there anything I can do to help?" Kelly asked.

"Why, yes, Kelly," Mrs. Collins said. Two dimples creased her rosy cheeks when she smiled.

"Will you put the plates and silverware on the table? Everyone is so busy dancing that I thought I would have to do all the work myself."

The two of them worked well together. Kelly enjoyed a detailed job when something was bothering her. It helped take her mind off the problem.

Mrs. Collins was short and plump. Her dark hair, coiled on top of her head, shone like polished mahogany. Her steps were quick, her movements exact. As she bustled around the room she pursed her lips, as if this made the job easier to accomplish.

In short order the table was laden with food, a tempting spread of meat and pickles, sandwiches and deviled eggs, yeast rolls and salads. And the desserts! Every one was tempting.

Kelly's stomach rumbled in anticipation. A piece of chicken would taste good now, she thought. But she waited for Mrs. Collins to call the dancers in, falling back to wait her turn at the table.

"Come on, Kelly," Mike invited her after heaping his plate with chicken and salad and two pieces of pie. "Let's go outdoors and eat. Come on, you kids, let's go this way." He motioned with a shake of his head.

Mike led the girls and Tim to the side of the building where they found split logs to sit on. The sun, now low in the sky, drenched the air with yellow light and threw long shadows across the rock-strewn yard.

"This is fun," Evelyn said, smiling directly at Kelly.

She's trying to make up, Kelly thought, returning a smile, but making it a little shorter and less friendly than the one she'd received. She hadn't quite forgiven Evelyn yet.

"I think I'd like to live here," Lucy said, taking her cue from her sister and looking to her for approval.

Evelyn raised her eyebrows.

"Well, maybe just in the summertime," Lucy added.

Tim said, "Then you'd miss the best part of living on the creeks. In the winter we go skiing and skating and sleigh riding."

"And hunting in the fall," Mike said. "Don't forget that."

"Girls wouldn't know anything about that," Tim answered.

"Kelly does," Mike said with a hint of praise in his voice.

"Oh, let's talk about something else," Evelyn interrupted. She daintily picked up a crumb from her plate and gazed at Tim. "Are you coming to Fairbanks for the Fourth of July celebration?"

"Sure, I guess so. I mean we always do."

"And you always stay with us," Evelyn added, flashing Tim a smile. He blushed right up to the roots of his hair.

"This year I'm going to win the fifty-yard

dash," Mike bragged, his crooked grin spreading from ear to ear. "There's a ten dollar prize!"

"You are?" challenged Tim. "That's the race I'm going to win."

"Show me right now," Mike said eagerly, brushing his blond hair away from his eyes. "I'll race you from here to the schoolhouse and back."

"Kelly, you start us," Tim said, crouching in a sprinting position. The girls moved back to one side.

Kelly stood behind the boys, not knowing which one she should root for. She wanted both of them to win.

"Ready, set, go!" she yelled.

Tim's long legs carried him forward fastest. But Mike was making good time behind him. Both runners were kicking up a lot of dust. They touched the side of the schoolhouse at the same time.

"Faster, Tim, faster!" Evelyn squealed.

"Hurry, Mike, hurry," Lucy cried, her voice pitched even higher than her sister's.

"Come on, Tim!" Kelly yelled. "Come on, Mike!"

Tim gave an extra burst of energy and spurted ahead over the finish line. He threw himself down on the grass to rest.

Mike was panting heavily when he reached the others. "I better practice more before the Fourth," he said. "I still think I can beat you."

Kelly noticed how sweat ran down his dusty, sun-browned cheeks.

"Hey," Tim said, "why don't you girls race?"

Tim and Mike looked at each other and laughed.

"Oh, let Lucy and Kelly," Evelyn said quickly. "I simply can't."

"I'll get my dress dirty," Lucy complained.

But Kelly said, "Oh, no you won't. Your dress isn't any longer than mine." She was eager to race. She could beat Lucy easily. She knew she could.

"Go on, Lucy," Mike said, giving her a playful shove. With that kind of persuasion, she had to follow Kelly to the starting line.

Ma'd have a fit if she saw her daughter racing, Kelly knew. And in her good shoes and dress, too. But Kelly didn't hesitate.

"Where do we run to?" Lucy asked.

"Down to the schoolhouse and back, just like the boys did," Kelly explained as if speaking to a small child.

"Everybody ready?" Tim asked, now up on his feet and ready to manage the race.

"Yes!" Kelly answered.

"I guess so," Lucy mumbled.

"On your mark," Tim yelled. "Get set, go!"

Kelly darted ahead. Her smooth-soled shoes were slippery in the soft sand. The wind blew through her hair and her ribbon slipped loose. She made herself run faster, although there was no need. Lucy was far behind.

At the schoolhouse, Kelly made a fast turn. She passed Lucy still going the other way.

"I don't think it's fair!" Lucy wailed. "I'm not used to running."

"Yea for Kelly, yea for Kelly!" both Mike and Tim were shouting when Kelly crossed the finish line. The winner!

"I'm not racing any more," Lucy shouted as she walked back, her feet dragging.

The boys laughed. They were satisfied, and it didn't surprise them to see Lucy give up.

But Evelyn spoke crossly, "Oh, act your age, Lucy. Come on, let's go back in the hall."

Mike walked beside Kelly, who was trying to retie the ribbon in her hair. "I'll bet you can win over all the Fairbanks girls at the Fourth of July races," he whispered.

His words redeemed the day. Kelly was happy.

8
Gold Fever

For two weeks after the dance the weather kept getting hotter and hotter. The thermometer at the store passed the ninety degree mark. There was no wind, not even a breeze to move the curtains hanging motionless in the open windows all over Gold City.

The bright sunlight sizzled on the tin roofs and baked the wooden sidewalks too hot for bare feet. The dogs, with red tongues hanging slack, took to the creeks several times a day with the children right behind them.

"How much longer can this heat last?" the people asked, fanning themselves with paper.

Kelly was in the store the day the rain came. She watched the brilliant dark blue clouds move overhead. A light wind raised the leaves on the uppermost branches of the trees and made the tall stalks of grasses sway.

She heard the hungry, dry sound of thunder, like an animal's roar, and she shrank back at the ferocious flashes of lightning whipping overhead.

Big drops of rain, round like pancakes, started splattering on hot tin and dry wood. The rain came faster, blown into open doors and windows by the wind, pouring out of the sky with such a great intensity that the ground could not drink it up fast enough.

Then the thunder seemed satisfied and gave off contented sounds, an occasional belching and a low, deep growling.

Kelly ran into the yard, letting the rain pound against her cheeks and soak her hair. The water running down her neck was a delight.

"Kelly, girl," Pa called, "what are you doing?" He stood in the doorway of the store, his dark apron wrapped around his middle, and watched her prance in the rain puddles in her bare feet.

"It's raining, it's raining," she laughed merrily.

"I can see that," he answered in a good-natured tone. "You'd better come in. You'll get cold."

"The rain is warm. It's really warm, Pa."

"Don't let your ma catch you," he said, but he didn't make her come in.

In a short while the rain stopped suddenly, just like that, and the sun was blazing hot again. The air was muggier than it had been before.

"Pa," Kelly called through the screen door, "can I walk to the mine and see Flapjack Charlie?"

"I guess it's all right," Pa's voice came from the back of the store. "Be home in time for dinner."

"I will."

Kelly had not clerked at the store since her run-in with Mrs. Turnbarge had been discovered. She had hinted more than once that she was ready to help out, but neither Ma nor Pa would allow it.

Kelly found her shoes and stockings on the wooden porch where she had peeled them off when the rain started. Her sleeveless dress was still damp from the rain.

I won't go in to change, Kelly decided. Ma will surely find some chore to do. That was Ma, never content to have anyone standing around idle. "If you can't find something to do, I'll find something for you." She always said that.

Away from the store, yellow-and-white-petaled wild daisies grew, iridescent from the rain. Kelly stopped long enough to pick a few blossoms and pin them in her hair.

"Ah, my pretty bambino!" Flapjack Charlie cried when Kelly pushed open the cookhouse door. He clapped his hands and cocked his head to one side to admire her. His face shone from the heat of the ovens where cinnamon-flavored apple pies were browning nicely.

"Flapjack, do you work all the time?" Kelly asked, stepping into the hot room.

100

"Lotsa work to do here, lotsa work," he said in his strong Italian accent.

A thick black moustache drooped above his lips, and his dark eyes darted in every direction. His body was lean, his movements energetic and brisk.

There was always that thump, thump of Charlie's wooden leg on the floor boards, a reminder of the time he froze his leg in a winter blizzard. That's when he lost it.

"I never meant to be a cook," Flapjack had told Kelly many times with a shrug of his bony shoulders. "But that's all I'm good for now."

Kelly sat at the table. "Flapjack, you are the noisiest cook," she said. "And about the best."

Flapjack rattled the lids of the pots and banged the oven door louder just because she was there. "Well, what is my pretty little girl up to today?"

Kelly thought of all the good times she had spent with Flapjack Charlie in the kitchen. She had helped him knead bread, peel potatoes—fifty-pound sacks—and chop onions until the tears ran down her face and plopped on the cutting board.

I'm going to miss him. I'm going to miss him, I'm going to miss him, Kelly thought with a sudden rush of tenderness. Her eyes misted with tears. She couldn't help it.

"Oh, Flapjack," she said, "I don't know what to do."

"What is it, little girl, what is it?" Flapjack Charlie reached out and touched her hand.

"We might have to leave Gold City," she blurted out, "and I don't want to go."

"Well," Flapjack said, leaning back in his chair, pulling on his suspenders. "I thought maybe somebody in your family die, you look so sad."

Kelly swallowed her tears. "I love Gold City," she said. "I don't want to live in Fairbanks." Then she told him the whole story—about the store and the dredging company. Flapjack listened, without speaking, nodding his head sympathetically from time to time.

"If I could earn enough money and help pay off the debts, then I'm sure Pa would stay here," Kelly told him. "But Tim says it's impossible. Ma won't talk about it, and Pa, well, he doesn't seem to care. I *have* to do something."

Flapjack Charlie clicked his tongue. That always meant he was thinking hard. "You wanna make money," he said, talking in that rapid fire way he had, "all the money you want, right outsida the door." He pointed his bony finger for emphasis.

Kelly looked out the door. She didn't see anything except trees and tailing piles.

"Tailing piles!" she said suddenly. "Gold!"

"Thatsa right," Flapjack nodded eagerly. "You can pan gold in the tailing piles."

After the miners sluiced the pay dirt, there was always gold dust and, if you were lucky, a few small nuggets to be found in the washed gravel, if you had the time and patience to pan it.

"I don't know why I never thought of that, Flapjack," Kelly said. "What a wonderful idea!" A frown creased her forehead. "You don't think Mr. Cooper will care if I pan on company property?"

Tim had told Kelly that Elias Cooper, foreman of the Exploration Company mine, was pretty touchy about strangers coming on the property. "He would just as soon shoot a man as ask questions," Tim had said.

"Don't you worry about that," Flapjack said. "Mr. Cooper, he's my friend. I'll take care of him."

"When can I start?" Kelly asked eagerly.

"Right now, kid, right now. I'll get you a gold pan." Flapjack rummaged in the cupboard while Kelly waited impatiently.

He finally found what he was looking for—a round, shallow metal pan with flared sides. "This is the one I used to use," Flapjack said, handing Kelly the well-worn pan.

"Thank you, Flapjack—I love you," she added impulsively and rushed out the door.

Kelly surveyed the tailing piles with a critical eye. Which one, she wondered, has the most gold in it? After a moment's hesitation, she decided to start with the pile near the stand of spindly aspen trees.

It took more than an hour to get everything ready. First she had to find the big washtub. Then she lugged water from the creek until the tub was more than half full. She shoveled a load of gravel from the tailing pile into the washtub.

After searching the area near the cookhouse, Kelly found an orange crate that would serve as a stool. She settled herself as comfortably as possible. She was ready.

Kelly dipped the gold pan into the tub. She scooped up water and gravel. First she picked out the large pieces of rock and threw them aside. With a practiced twist of the wrists, just like Harry had taught her, Kelly swished the water over the top of the dirt to wash away the small particles.

With a continuous rotating motion Kelly swirled the water over the top of the pan and poured it back into the tub with the excess dirt. Then she dipped into the tub for more water.

Dip, swish, pour. Dip, swish, pour. That was the refrain that kept running through Kelly's mind as she worked. Dip, swish, pour. It gave a rhythm to the task.

At last she began to see something, tiny flakes of gold, at the bottom of the pan. She was so excited she nearly fell into the tub. Careful now! She swirled the water to carry off the remaining dirt. Then she poured off the water.

There was her first gold—tiny flecks clustered in the bottom of the pan. Kelly ran to the cookhouse.

"Look, Flapjack," she cried. "Gold!"

Flapjack moved quickly to her side. "Ahhh!" he said, his eyes going shiny black, "you gotta the gold!"

They laughed together.

"Do you have anything I can put the gold in?" she asked.

Flapjack found a small jar. "Fill it up," he said.

Kelly went back to her gold mine. If she could just get enough gold today to cover the bottom of the glass jar, she would be happy.

In the hot sun she worked, unaware of the mosquitoes buzzing around her head, of the fat bees sucking honey from the wild roses and bluebells, or the translucent-winged dragonflies setting a zig-zag course over the tops of the wild grasses.

Sweat was running down her neck, her hands were freezing from dipping them in the cold water. Her back and shoulders ached from leaning over the tub. Was the orange crate ever uncomfortable! Just a little longer, Kelly told herself. I'll do one more pan and then I'll go home. Just one more pan.

"Kelly, what are you doing here?" It was Tim's voice.

Kelly raised her head. Her face was dirt smudged. Her dress was wet down the front. She had removed her wet stockings an hour ago, much to the delight of the mosquitoes.

"Tim, is that you?" she asked questioningly, squinting both eyes. Tim was a black figure in the glare of the sun.

"Of course it's me. What are you doing here? You're a mess."

"I'm panning gold," she said excitedly. "Look!" She held up the glass jar. The bottom was nearly covered with gold flakes. "I panned all that this afternoon."

Tim held the jar. "It isn't very much," he said. He was used to seeing the thick collection of gold nuggets caught in the sluice boxes at the mine. This was pretty slim pickings as far as he was concerned. "You probably have less than a quarter of an ounce," he said. "It's only worth about six dollars."

"Six dollars!" Kelly said, "I think that's pretty good. Besides, tomorrow I'll do better. Maybe I'll even get some nuggets."

Tim shook his head. "I think I know what you are up to, Kelly, but it won't work. You can't pan enough gold this way. All the heavy gold has been mined out of this gravel."

"I don't care what you say," she shouted. "You know I don't want to go to Fairbanks. You don't care one bit how *I* feel. You are mean and selfish. All you ever do is make fun of everything I do."

Kelly was too mad to cry. She had worked so hard this day and felt so excited about what she was doing. Then Tim came along and spoiled everything.

Tim stepped back. Kelly had never shouted at

him like that before. "I'm going home now," he said coldly. "Are you coming?"

"No," she answered sullenly, starting to work another pan.

"You'll be late for dinner."

"I don't care."

"I'm going." He was offering her a second chance to go with him.

"Go ahead." She didn't look up. She heard him walk away. "And don't you dare tell Ma and Pa what I'm doing," she shouted after him.

"Don't worry about it." His tone was as unfriendly as her own.

She bent her head over her work. The sun still blazed. The hour melted away.

Suddenly Kelly stood up, the gold pan clattered to the ground. She had to get home. Oh, dear, she had to get home. She hadn't planned to stay this long.

When she slipped into her place at the dinner table the family had already started eating. Both Ma and Pa disapproved of her tardiness. They wouldn't let her go on like this, she knew that. She would make the best of it while she could.

That wasn't the only night Kelly was late for dinner. Every night the rest of the week was like that. She would leave the house early in the morning as soon as Pa went to work and Ma was weeding in the garden. It was after seven in the evening when she returned.

If Ma and Pa knew what she was up to, they didn't say anything to her about it. Maybe they thought it was good for her to get things worked out for herself.

Sometimes Kelly would remember to make a sandwich to take with her for lunch, but when she forgot (and that was often), Flapjack Charlie was always there offering fresh baked cinnamon rolls or a slice of pie hot out of the oven.

Every day Kelly cared less and less about the way she looked. Any dress would do, the older the better. She braided her hair because it was easier that way, and cooler. Red welts covered her wrists and arms where the mosquitoes had feasted. Her hands were rough and red. Vaseline didn't help smooth them anymore. Kelly didn't care. The gold flakes climbing higher and higher up the side of the jar were what mattered to her.

She felt driven to the gold mine by a strong force. Even though she was exhausted at the end of each day, she couldn't stay away. Every night she slept hard, without dreaming. She was wide awake at exactly six o'clock every morning, eager to get started again, wondering how much gold she would pan that day.

"I think our kid has gotta the gold fever," Flapjack Charlie would say to no one in particular as he watched Kelly's dark head bent over the gold pan, her blue eyes peering anxiously for gold. "Yup, she's got the gold fever."

110

9
Pa Speaks Out

"Where are you going, Kelly?" Ma called from the garden where she was down on her knees thinning carrots.

Kelly hesitated on the back porch, letting the screen door close quietly. She had hoped to slip out before Ma spotted her. "I'm going to Harry's," she answered. "I have something to give him."

Ma didn't answer right away. Kelly waited, crossing her fingers in hopes that Ma wouldn't make her stay home. Tucked under her arm was the glass jar of gold dust, carefully wrapped in a woolen scarf. She had been hiding the gold in her dresser drawer, under her stockings. Today she was planning to take the jar to Harry's cabin. She would ask him to keep it safe for her.

"Don't stay too long," Ma said finally, "I need some help in the garden today."

Kelly made a face she didn't think Ma could see. "All right," she said, not too enthusiastically. She left the yard quickly before Ma changed her mind and made her do the gardening first.

She stopped at the store. The bell over the door rang sharply as she entered.

"I'll be right with you," Pa called from the back room.

"It's just me, Pa," Kelly said.

On the counter next to the cash register stood the glass jars of candy—each filled with a different kind. There were peppermint sticks, fat yellow butterscotch balls, root beer balls, licorice whips, cinnamon sticks, and sour balls. Kelly dipped into the licorice jar and took three sticks.

"Stop, thief!" Pa said, coming up behind her and grabbing her by the shoulders.

"Ohhh," Kelly cried, "you scared me, Pa." She hiked the jar of gold dust higher under her arm.

"Why are you eating candy so early in the morning?" Pa wanted to know. "Didn't you eat your breakfast?"

"I ate breakfast," Kelly answered. It wasn't exactly a lie. She had eaten. One slice of bread with butter and jam—she was so anxious to be on her way. "I'm going to Harry's," she said, making her way to the door. "I'll be back pretty soon."

Pa smiled at her eagerness to be off.

She was gone before Pa could tell her that Mrs. Turnbarge had paid her bill—in full. That would make Kelly happy, Pa knew. But these days, Kelly never seemed to be in one place long enough to hear the news.

For Kelly it was a special pleasure to be out walking early in the day like this before people began to stir and break the sweet silence of the morning. The air was clear and tingling as fresh running creek water. It would be easy, Kelly imagined, to reach out and touch the top of the summit.

Along the road the leaves hung gray and limp, covered with dust from passing wagon wheels. Kelly came to an open field where lightning had once set the dry grasses aflame. Now the field was ablaze with fireweed, magenta-colored flowers swaying on two-foot high stalks. Fireweed is one of the first plants to revive the earth after a fire, bringing a bright badge of hope in its deep red blossoms.

Small rabbits in their summer brindle-brown coats dashed across the path from time to time. They seemed to know Kelly wouldn't hurt them. Sometimes the rabbits got halfway across the path, stopped, wiggled their noses, and then made a sudden burst for cover. Their padded feet made soft noises in the dry spruce needles and last year's cranberry leaves.

Hundreds of dandelions grew around Harry's cabin. He never cut them. In a few weeks the yellow-flowered weeds would be a foot or more high.

"We'll make dandelion wine someday," Harry promised as he did every year.

Harry had built his cabin from the fine tall timber on his property. The walls were made of logs, stacked one on top of the other. In the narrow spaces between the logs, moss was packed for insulation.

The cabin had a sod roof where more weeds grew and a small birch tree got its start. The heat inside the cabin warmed the sod, and a lush crop of chickweeds and dandelions grew from the roof even before the ground below was fully thawed. The miners on Walnut Creek, methodical men that they were, scattered lettuce and radish seeds on their sod roofs. They were the first ones to have a summer salad.

Over the front door where the roof pitched, Harry had nailed a pair of moose antlers. The bleached rack spread open like huge hands to welcome a guest inside.

Harry came around the side of the cabin. "Hello, Kelly," he greeted her happily. "Haven't seen much of you for a while. What have you been up to?"

As they walked into the cabin, Kelly told him in a great rush of words about her gold panning at the mine. They sat facing each other at the kitchen table. Harry listened intently, sipping black coffee from a chipped mug and nodding his head at appropriate times.

Kelly unwrapped the glass jar she had carried so carefully from home. "See how much I've panned," she said proudly. But as she spoke, the pile of gold dust seemed smaller to her for some reason. She guessed that she had talked her accomplishment up bigger than it really was.

"I see," Harry said, turning the jar this way and that, letting the sun cast light on the tiny particles of gold. "Ummm. Very good. What are you going to do with your treasure?"

"Didn't I tell you?" Kelly asked excitedly, the color rushing to her cheeks in two red spots. "I am going to save Pa's store! He still is talking about selling out to the dredging company. If I can get enough money to pay the bills and get more stock, then we can stay."

Harry frowned. "That's a pretty big undertaking, Kelly," he said. There was sympathy in those kind blue eyes.

"I know," she agreed quickly, "but if I can keep working as hard as I've worked this past week, I can make it. I just know I can. And maybe the next tailing pile will be even better."

Harry couldn't help but laugh. "Spoken like a true miner," he said, clapping his hands. "What can I do to help you?"

"Will you let me leave my gold in your cabin? I want this to be a surprise for Ma and Pa."

"Oh, they don't know about this? I see," Harry said, nodding his shiny bald head. He left the table and came back with a moosehide poke, a narrow leather pouch with a drawstring at the top. "Let's put the gold in this," he said. "We don't want to take the chance of breaking the jar and losing the gold."

"Good idea," Kelly said, holding the poke open

116

while Harry poured in the gold dust. "How much do you think it's worth?" she asked eagerly, her eyes shiny with expectancy.

Harry weighed the poke in his hands. "I'd say it must be worth at least thirty dollars."

"Is that all?" Kelly said, a trifle disappointed. After all those hours of bending over the washtub, dunking her hands in the cold water, and doing the dip, swish, pour routine over and over, Kelly thought she had made at least a hundred dollars.

"You have to remember," Harry said, "that that gravel has already been panned. It takes a long time to make any money with just gold dust."

Kelly nodded her head. That's what Tim had been trying to tell her. Well, she wouldn't let that stop her. She would just work harder and faster and longer. Determination welled up inside her. "I have to go," she said suddenly. "I have lots of panning to do."

"Hold your horses," Harry said, putting a hand on her shoulder. "Mike is loading the wagon to deliver wood to the mine. You can ride with him."

"All right," Kelly agreed, walking out the door with Harry.

"I'll put your poke under the floorboards of the cabin," Harry said quietly. "It will be safe there."

It wasn't until Kelly and Mike were driving past the store that Kelly remembered she was supposed to help Ma with the gardening.

Oh, no, she thought, I don't want to work in

the garden. She opened her mouth to tell Mike to stop, but the words didn't come out. They rode past her house. Kelly shut her mouth without speaking. She didn't see Ma in the yard. So far she was safe. She wouldn't stay too long at the mine, she promised herself.

Mike stopped the horses at the tailing pile Kelly pointed out. "That's my mining operation," Kelly said importantly.

"You really must like to pan for gold if you are willing to go through that washed pay dirt," Mike said. "That's the hard way to do it."

"I don't mind," Kelly said, "I am doing it for a very good reason." She didn't intend to tell Mike any more than that.

Mike helped carry the water from the creek to the washtub where Kelly was already swishing her pan through the water.

Mike watched her for a few minutes before he spoke. "Why don't you use a rocker instead of the gold pan? It would be a lot faster."

"I never thought of that," Kelly admitted, looking up at him. "Is there a rocker around here I could use?"

"I saw one over by the bunkhouse."

"Let's go find it."

The rocker was still there, leaning against the bunkhouse, partially covered with weeds. It was a boxy affair, standing about two feet high, with a wide trough in front. Because it was built on rockers like a rocking chair, the miners could shake it back and forth to sift the gold from the gravel.

"I wonder if we can move it?" Kelly said, putting her shoulder against the rocker. No, it was too heavy for her.

"What's going on here?" a man's voice said behind them.

Kelly and Mike turned to face Mr. Cooper, the company foreman. The way he stood, feet planted firmly apart on the ground, arms folded across his chest, made Mike and Kelly feel like trespassers.

Mike was the first to speak. "You see, sir," he started out, "we were looking at this rocker."

"You know that's company property, don't you?" the man asked. Mr. Cooper was broad-shouldered with a thick, red neck, but his short, spindly

legs made him look top-heavy. His iron-gray hair grew wildly around his face, and in the back it disappeared in a curly swirl below his collar.

We are in for it now, Kelly thought.

Mike spoke, "I thought it would be easier for Kelly to use the rocker instead of the gold pan for mining."

"What mining?" Mr. Cooper demanded, looking from Mike to Kelly and back to Mike again. "What's going on around here?"

"Didn't Flapjack Charlie tell you?" Kelly asked anxiously. "He said it would be all right if I panned the tailing piles."

Mr. Cooper burst out laughing. "Oh, are you the one?" he asked, pointing at Kelly as if she had something wrong with her. "Well, anyone who is willing to pan the tailing piles needs all the help she can get. Come on, young fellow," he said to Mike, "you can take one end and I'll take the other, and we'll carry this thing over for the young lady."

Kelly led the way, not quite sure how to take Mr. Cooper's abrupt change in attitude. Tim had told her that he was unpredictable. The men at the mine tried to stay clear of him, never knowing when he would erupt in anger.

"Let's put it here under the trees," Mr. Cooper said. "No need to have the little lady sunburn her nose."

Kelly didn't know how to react to his kindness. She always got along with people older than herself, but Mr. Cooper wasn't like anybody she'd ever met before.

As soon as the rocker was in place, Mike said hurriedly, "I guess I'd better be going. I have to unload the wagon. I'll see you, Kelly." And he was off.

Kelly wished she could run after him. She wanted to say, "Don't leave me alone with Mr. Cooper."

"Now, Kelly," Mr. Cooper said in his most businesslike voice, "I will show you how to operate the rocker."

Kelly almost blurted out, "I know how to work the rocker," but she thought better of it.

"This top part is called the hopper, and the hopper is where you put the gravel." Mr. Cooper illustrated by filling the hopper with a load from the tailing pile. "Then you take a dipper full of water," he said as he scooped some water from the washtub, "and pour it over the gravel while you rock the rocker back and forth, like a baby's cradle." He was so pleased with this comparison that he smiled broadly. "The dirt will be washed down through the holes in the hopper to the canvas pockets in the next section." He looked at Kelly to see if she was following all this.

Kelly nodded her head to let him know she was keeping up with him.

"The gold—if you are lucky enough to get any working the tailing piles—will get caught in the canvas pockets. The gold flakes will sift down to the bottom section and get caught in the riffles.

"You won't need to clean the canvas pockets and riffles very often," he continued, "because you aren't going to get that much gold. Here, try your hand at it."

Kelly took the handle of the rocker and pushed. Nothing happened.

"You are going to have to work a lot harder than that," Mr. Cooper said. He placed his hand over hers and helped her push back and forth.

"It isn't as easy as I thought it was going to be," Kelly admitted. Even with Mr. Cooper's help the rocker was hard to move.

"You'll get used to it," he said, handing her the dipper. "Don't forget, you have to pour water over the gravel as you rock or it won't work." He stood back to watch her.

It took Kelly a few minutes to get the rocker working right. She pushed with all the strength she had in her right arm and poured water with the left. The rocker screeched over the rocks on the ground. It took all her might to move the thing, but she had to prove to Mr. Cooper that she could do it.

"That's pretty good," Mr. Cooper said at last. "I think you'll make it all right. I'll be back later."

Kelly was glad when he was gone. Sweat ran down her neck. The muscles in her arms and back rebelled at the strenuous job. Even the bottoms of her feet hurt. Kelly heaved a deep sigh and put her hand on the rocker. She forced herself to work. If she could only keep it up she could wash five, maybe ten times more gravel this way than with the gold pan. She wanted so badly to find the pockets inside the rocker filled with gold. It would be hard to resist the temptation to look inside the rocker every few minutes to see how much money she had made.

The sun sailed across the cloud-scattered sky. Kelly continued to work, forgetful of the time. One more load, she kept saying to herself. One more load. She couldn't stop.

Kelly's stomach growled in hunger. That single piece of bread, eaten hours ago, had long worn off. At midafternoon Flapjack Charlie brought her a moose meat sandwich, cold tea, and a wide slice of pumpkin pie. Kelly fell on the food without persuasion. How good it tasted! She leaned against the tree while she ate.

"Flapjack," she said grandly, "I am going to be very, very rich. I will buy all my friends wonderful presents."

Flapjack chuckled as he made his way back to the cookhouse. "Don't count those chickens before they hatch," he said over his shoulder.

The day lengthened into evening. It was then Kelly dared to look inside the canvas pockets of the rocker. Nuggets! She saw nuggets. Not very big ones, mind you, but they were nuggets just the same. "Whooopee!" Kelly shouted out loud, even though there was no one to hear her. She scooped the nuggets in her hand and held them with amazement.

Did I do all that? she thought. Did I really do all that? She dropped the gold into the glass jar. The gold dust caught in the riffles would have to wait until tomorrow. Kelly cast an anxious glance at the sky. It was late. Very late. No matter how fast she ran she would be in for it now.

The screen door creaked noisily as Kelly pushed it open. Ma, Pa, and Tim were seated at the kitchen table. When Tim saw Kelly he excused himself and left the room. That's a bad sign, Kelly decided.

No one spoke while Kelly washed in the tin basin on the washstand. Long shafts of yellow sunlight slanted into the kitchen and gleamed on the polished stove. After the fire got low Ma wiped the stove top with a rag and ran a piece of candle wax over the top to give it extra sheen.

"Your dinner is cold," Ma said.

"That's all right," Kelly answered brightly, trying to make her voice sound casual. She spooned a few cold peas on her plate. Pa passed the mashed potatoes. There was one caribou chop left for her. She didn't like caribou, but she wouldn't complain about it. Not tonight she wouldn't.

"I thought I told you to come right home from Harry's," Ma said, getting right to the subject.

"I know you did, Ma," Kelly started to explain, "but when I got there Mike was taking the wagon to the mine and he asked if I wanted to ride along. I only planned to stay a few minutes, but I found this rocker and started to mine and I just couldn't stop." She knew she hadn't told it very well, but that was the best she could do.

"That is no excuse," Ma said. "You knew you were supposed to be home and you deliberately disobeyed me."

Kelly swallowed hard. She knew Ma was right, but Ma didn't understand how important the gold mining was to her. She said, "I am sorry, Ma," and it occurred to her that she seemed to be saying that a lot lately.

Then Ma started to mention all the things Kelly had forgotten to do in the past weeks. "Your room is a mess," she was saying, "you haven't helped in the garden or with the laundry. You don't carry any water up from the creek, you never do the breakfast dishes, and you are always late for dinner."

Pa's face grew more disapproving as Kelly's faults were aired. Finally he spoke. "You will not go to the mine for a week," he said. "I want you to stay here and help your ma."

"A whole week! Oh, Pa."

"You heard me," he said, pushing his chair away from the table. "I'm going to the store," he said to Ma. The screen door banged behind him.

Kelly sat with her elbows on the table, her head in her hands. A whole week. She nearly cried.

10
The Worst Week

Kelly would remember it as The Worst Week That Ever Was. Ma found plenty of work for her to do, but it wasn't the work that she minded. It was being away from the mine—that was the part that really hurt.

Every day as Kelly busied herself with weeding the garden, beating the rugs, washing lamp chimneys, airing blankets, and sewing on buttons, she thought how she could be rocking more gold out of the gravel.

She didn't ask to visit Harry. She wanted to show him the nuggets, but that would have to wait. A week had never seemed so long before.

By the fourth day Ma was running out of things for Kelly to do, although she wouldn't admit it.

"Why don't you sit in the sun and read a book?" Ma suggested after they finished washing the windows inside and out.

"Are you sure there isn't anything else you want me to do?" Kelly asked, trying to be helpful.

"No," Ma replied, "I don't want you to work all the time. Summer is for being lazy and enjoying yourself." They sat in the kitchen sipping iced tea. "After this week is over, I don't want you spending a lot of time at the mine. That work is too hard for you."

"But, Ma," Kelly protested, "I love being at the mine. And the work isn't that hard, really it isn't."

Ma brushed the damp hair away from her face. She always looked the same to Kelly, that wonderful, dark, shiny hair piled on top of her head, her skin clear and pink all the time. She will never get old, will she? Kelly wondered. She couldn't imagine Ma ever changing. She was always the same.

But now Ma's face took on a serious look, and Kelly knew a lecture was coming.

"There are some things we have to learn to accept," Ma said.

Kelly's heart beat faster. Don't let her say it, she prayed.

"And the possibility of moving to Fairbanks is one of them."

Ma had said it. The subject was out in the open now. Ma had accepted the idea. That meant Pa was in on it, too. Tim, well, Kelly knew how he felt. She was the only one resisting the idea. Kelly was hopelessly outnumbered. She perched on the edge of the kitchen chair.

"We haven't made a definite decision to sell the store yet," Ma said, "but you must face the fact that we might move into Fairbanks."

Kelly felt defeated. There was a hollow place inside her.

"If Pa got a lot of money, wouldn't that help?"

"It isn't likely Pa will get a lot of money."

Kelly wanted to tell Ma that she would have a lot of money by September, if only they would wait. But she thought of the thirty dollars in gold dust and the handful of nuggets. That was not a lot of money, not yet anyway.

"Living in Fairbanks won't be so bad," Ma was saying. "Pa won't have to work such long hours, Tim will attend a better school, and you will meet lots of girls your own age."

"I don't see why girls my own age are so important," Kelly insisted. "I'd much rather go fishing with Harry than do all those silly things girls think are so much fun. I don't care about meeting girls my own age."

Ma reached for Kelly's hand. "That's how you feel now, dear, but when you get to Fairbanks, you will feel differently about it."

Kelly could not have agreed with her less, but she did not say so. "I guess I will go read a book," she said instead.

With a book in one hand and an old blanket in the other, Kelly made her way to the banks of Crooked Creek. It was one of those just-right warm days with a delicious breeze off the water to temper the heat of the sun.

Tiny bluebells, fringed in pink, nodded along the creek bank where Kelly spread the blanket. She lay on her stomach, her book under her nose, reading *Heidi* for the third time. The melody of the creek water, the soothing purr of the breeze, and the gentle warmth of sunlight lulled Kelly to sleep.

Ma found her sleeping an hour later. "Kelly," she said, gently shaking her by the shoulder. "Wake up, dear."

Kelly lifted her head and stared with blank, sleep-shrouded eyes. "Whaaat?"

"Wake up," Ma repeated. "I have to go to Sara City. Mrs. Portman's baby came early and she wants me to help her. I am going to stay overnight. You will have to fix supper for Pa and Tim. I've told Pa about it."

Kelly pushed herself into a sitting position. It seemed as if she had been sleeping a long time. Her head was twirling. She blinked her eyes again and again. Things were beginning to come into focus. "When are you leaving?" Her voice was thick and husky.

"Right away," Ma answered. "Walt is waiting for me. I'll be back tomorrow. I am sure you can manage." She kissed Kelly on the cheek.

Kelly watched Ma's retreating figure, back straight like a dancer's, head held high, and footsteps light and quick. "Good-bye, Ma," Kelly called.

Ma turned, waved, and then she was gone.

The house wasn't the same without Ma. Kelly noticed it the minute she stepped into the kitchen. The liveliness her presence brought to the house was missing. Kelly could feel it in the air. She could see it in the way the curtains hung limp at the windows, in the way the chairs stood empty at an odd angle from the table.

Kelly was restless. There was plenty of time before Pa would be home for dinner, she decided. Surely there was enough time to make his favorite biscuits. She was still mixing the dough when Tim came banging in the back door.

"Why are you home so early?" Kelly wanted to know.

"It isn't early. It's after five."

"It is? Oh, no! How did it get so late? What time is Pa coming home for dinner?"

"In about half an hour. And he said to tell you that he is bringing someone home with him."

Kelly pulled her hands out of the biscuit dough. "You mean someone for dinner?"

"Yup."

"I'll never be ready," Kelly wailed, vigorously rolling out the dough. "Who's coming?"

Tim turned away as if he wasn't going to tell her.

"Who is it?" she repeated, determined to get the information out of him now because he had hesitated.

"No one you know," was his answer as he started out the door.

Kelly was right behind him, rolling pin in hand. "Tell me who it is," she demanded.

Tim had seen that determined look in her eyes before. He might just as well give in now as later.

"John Winslow."

"Who is that?"

"The man from the dredging company."

Kelly took a step backward. "Oh," she said. "What is he doing here?"

"Talking to Pa."

Kelly didn't have to ask what they were talking about. She knew. It was the store. And Pa was bringing that man home for dinner. Kelly boiled up inside. It wasn't fair. It just wasn't fair, she thought. How could Pa do this?

"You'll have to help me, Tim," Kelly said as he started out the door. Here she was up to her elbows in flour, nothing started for dinner, and the table wasn't even set.

"I'm tired," Tim said, "I worked all day."

"Please," Kelly pleaded. She was desperate. It was important to her that she make it the best dinner possible. She would show this Mr. Winslow that the Hansens knew how to do a thing or two.

Tim came to help her, as she knew he would.

Between them they served a meal that would have made Ma proud—moose meat sausages, boiled potatoes, leaf lettuce from the garden with oil and vinegar, pickled beets canned from last year's crop, and homemade biscuits with raspberry jam. For dessert, there was almond-flavored pound cake, which Kelly had to admit Ma made before she left that afternoon. Coffee came piping hot from the pot just the way Ma had taught Kelly to do.

"You have a mighty fine cook there," Mr. Winslow said, pushing his chair from the table and leisurely sipping his coffee.

Kelly had made up her mind to dislike Mr. Winslow even before she met him. Wasn't it partly his fault that they might sell the store and move away? Wasn't he threatening the things she loved the most? Didn't she have every right to dislike him?

Despite her intentions, Kelly found it hard to bear a grudge against this man with the quiet voice and the deep, honest laugh that brightened his lined face.

"You know, Kelly," Mr. Winslow said, addressing her directly for the first time, "Gold City is going to be a big town one of these days, maybe even bigger than Fairbanks."

Pa and Tim exchanged glances. "I like Gold City just the way it is," Kelly answered, meeting Mr. Winslow's direct gaze. "I don't want Gold City to change," she continued boldly.

Mr. Winslow nodded his head. So that was why she had not spoken all evening. Now he understood. "I used to feel that way a long time ago," he told her, "but then I discovered that everything was changing except me, and I didn't want to be left behind." He smiled as if he was thinking back to that time. "That will happen to you, too."

Kelly squirmed in her chair. They were waiting for her to say something, but she couldn't think of a thing polite enough. Mr. Winslow covered the awkward moment by saying, "What do you want to be when you grow up, Kelly?"

Funny, Kelly thought, no one ever asked me that before. She answered honestly, letting herself be drawn into the conversation. "I don't know. I haven't thought about it very much. Maybe a teacher."

"Then you will probably go to school in Seattle."

Kelly pulled back. Wait a minute, she thought, I haven't even gotten used to the idea of going to school in Fairbanks. Mr. Winslow, you go too fast. The way he said things made them sound like the easiest thing in the world. Go to school in Seattle, just like that. She had never considered such a thing for herself. For Tim, maybe, but not for her.

"I don't see why everyone is in such a hurry to get me out of Gold City," Kelly argued. "I don't see anything wrong with staying here."

Pa started to speak, but he let Mr. Winslow answer her. "There isn't anything wrong with Gold City," he said pleasantly, smoothly. "It's just that sometimes we outgrow a place, and it's time to move on."

"I haven't outgrown Gold City," she said. How could he say such a thing when she loved it so?

"Maybe you have, but you just don't know it."

"All I know," Kelly said, and her eyes were smarting, "is just when you get to liking something it is taken away from you."

"And something better is put in its place," Mr. Winslow added as if that was the way Kelly wanted to finish her sentence.

Kelly raised her small, pointed chin. Mr. Winslow was smiling, and when she saw his face, she had to smile, too. How could he make her smile when she didn't want to?

"I don't know about that," Kelly said, not willing to give in.

"When you have lived as long as I have," Mr. Winslow continued, "you will be able to look back on these things and see that they are true."

Their conversation ended there, but Kelly continued to think about his words while she washed the dishes. She didn't even ask Tim to stay and help clean up. She wanted to do it alone.

Something inside Kelly made her aware that what Mr. Winslow had said held special meaning for her. She let his words sift through her thoughts again and again, trying to get used to them.

He had said . . . *Everything is changing except me . . . and I won't want to be left behind . . . Sometimes we outgrow a place and it's time to move on . . .*

I don't want to think about it anymore, Kelly decided suddenly when the dishes were dried and put away. I want to stay in Gold City. I do not want to go to Fairbanks. I must get back to the mine to do more gold panning. I'll have to work hard to make up this lost week.

Kelly was in her bed, quilt pulled high on her chest, listening to the stirring of the willows outside her window when she heard Pa and Tim return from the store.

They were restless without Ma, too. She was the center around which all things revolved in that house. With Ma gone, they were like a watch without a mainspring, everyone popping off in a different direction and no one getting any place at all.

Tomorrow Ma will be back, Kelly thought drowsily, and everything will be the same again.

11
Fairbanks for the Fourth

Waiting seven whole days to go to the mine was hard enough, but now Kelly found she had to wait even longer. This is the way it happened.

Her first day of freedom fell on the Fourth of July. The Hansens always celebrated in grand style at the gala events scheduled in Fairbanks. Kelly was torn between the excitement of the holiday and her desire to return to the mine. When she reasoned the mine would always be there but the Fourth was only once a year, it wasn't hard to give in to the idea of celebration.

On the morning of the Fourth, the alarm clock sounded early and there was no lying in bed for an extra minute or two. Preparations began right away for the Hansens' holiday trip to Fairbanks.

As was their custom, they would stay overnight with the Bramsteads. Kelly wasn't exactly looking forward to that part, but there would be fun times—the parade, the races and the prizes, the baseball game, the horse races, and boating on the river. Late at night, even though it wouldn't get dark at all, there would be the fireworks display. Bigger, brighter, louder than last year was the promise. It was enough to send shivers of anticipation up and down Kelly's spine.

She couldn't hide her excitement as she ran from job to job, hurrying everyone as best she could.

"How many races are you going to win this year?" Pa asked Kelly. There was a twinkle in his eyes as he spoke.

"I'm going to win at least one," Kelly said confidently. She put a box filled with Ma's cranberry relish and rose hip syrup in the back of the wagon. Ma never went to anybody's house empty-handed. That was the way of the North. "I've been chasing a lot of rabbits to keep in practice," Kelly added.

That tickled Pa. It was a joke between them. A year ago when Kelly won twenty dollars in running races, someone asked Pa how Kelly had learned to be so fast on her feet. "Every morning she chases down a rabbit for breakfast," Pa had answered. That had embarrassed Kelly last year. Now she thought it was funny. Maybe I am changing, she decided.

"How many races are you going to enter, Tim?" Kelly asked her brother.

"Oh, I don't know. A couple, maybe. I want to give the other guys a chance." He slipped the halter over Dolly's head with a practiced hand. Tim did his work smoothly, his movements clean and brisk.

"That's nice of you," Kelly said with a smile. "I'm not going to be that generous. I want to win as many prizes as I can."

Kelly had it all figured out. If she could win first prize in the fifty-yard dash, and second prize in three other races, she would have more money than if she went mining today. The thought was consoling.

"Winning isn't everything," Pa said. Every once in a while, Pa came up with these "lesson sermons" as Kelly called them. They always seemed to be the opposite of what Kelly was thinking. Winning isn't everything. Well, why not? What could be more important, Kelly wanted to know. She didn't ask though. She didn't want to waste time in conversation. She wanted to be on the trail—right now.

Pa and Tim finished hitching up the horses. Dolly and Bravo yanked their heads in anticipation of the trip. Walt would drive the Hansens to the railroad siding in time to catch the first train to town. On the Fourth of July the mines closed. It was the only time during the whole summer that that happened. Everybody, well, practically everybody except Walt and a few stay-at-homes, went to Fairbanks. Extra passenger cars, some of them open flatbeds with wooden chairs, were added to the train to accommodate all the people traveling to the same place at the same time.

"I'll go and see if Ma is ready," Kelly said. She couldn't stay in one spot very long. She was eager to leave.

"Need any help?" Kelly asked Ma, dipping her finger into the egg salad mixture.

"Not that kind of help," Ma answered, waving Kelly away from the table. Ma was fixing a big lunch to carry on the train.

Kelly hoped they could sit in the open car. It was more fun that way with the wind rushing through your hair and pressing your eyes closed as the scenery slipped by and the train clickety-clacked along the rails.

Ma didn't like the open cars. One year a spark from the train settled on a lady's net hat and set it on fire. There was always that possibility, Kelly thought, but nothing like that ever happens when I'm around.

At last the wagon was loaded and waiting out front. The house was locked, windows closed. If they had forgotten anything, it was too late now. Pa never turned back once he started down the trail. Yellow puffs of dust followed the wagon wheels. The Hansens were on their way.

"We're the first ones ready," Kelly said from the back of the wagon where she and Tim found comfortable spots on an old quilt. "The Thorgaards haven't even left yet." She tried to be discreet about checking Mike's cabin, but Tim wouldn't let her get by that easily.

"Mike and his dad went to town last night," he said, "so you don't need to look for him."

Kelly tossed her head. "Who's looking?" she asked loftily, but it didn't fool Tim.

"You are," he said, yanking her braids.

Kelly poked him in the ribs with her elbow. Tim grinned good-naturedly and clasped his hands behind his head. His feet in big boots stuck out five inches beyond her high-button shoes.

"This is the life," Tim said with a sigh of contentment. His voice sounded more and more like Pa's every day.

The rhythmic jogging of the wagon, the scrape-scrape of the wheels over the rocks put Kelly in a drowsy mood. But there was no chance of getting any sleep because they were traveling the "washboard" road as Pa called it.

When Kelly was younger she thought Pa meant they would ride over real washboards, like Ma used to scrub the clothes. Pa explained how the deep furrows the wheels made when the road was muddy dried to form hard ridges that rippled the road. It didn't matter whether Pa took the ruts fast or slow, it was bumpy. The wagon squealed in every seam.

Despite the piling up of puffy gray-white clouds along the horizon, the sky held promise of a fine day. It was still cool, as it always was in the early, early morning, but that would pass as the sun rose steadily in the sky. By noon in Fairbanks the wooden planks of the grandstands erected along the riverfront would be warm to the touch. The band players, in tight-fitting white uniforms with gold braid, would step lively to their own music, their faces glistening from the heat.

The railroad siding was deserted when Pa reined the horses in beside the track. The train from Chatanika was due in twenty minutes, but it would be late today, sure as shooting, waiting for all the holiday passengers to board.

Kelly was never sure whether she saw the black smudge of smoke on the horizon first or felt the rumble along the ground before the iron engine came panting into view. It didn't matter. Bells ringing, whistle tooting, cinders falling, that was all part of the act when the train came over the top of the hill. By then all the Gold City people were there, standing in the boot-high weeds, waiting to board.

At the last minute the Bonovich wagon came racing up to the platform. "You wait! You wait!" Mrs. Bonovich yelled, shaking her first at the conductor, while she pushed her children ahead of her. Mr. Bonovich, a tall, bony-shouldered man, hitched the horses and followed in his wife's shadow, never speaking a word.

Women in long white summer dresses with wide-brimmed flowered hats and parasols, and men in dark narrow suits with tight white collars, waved from the train windows and open cars, calling greetings to friends.

Young girls in dresses trimmed with eyelet and lace ignored young boys in long pants and starched shirts. Before the trip was over, the boys and girls would be playing in the aisles.

"Pa," Kelly said, pulling on his arm, "can we sit in an open car?"

"It isn't very safe," he answered. "We had better find a place inside."

Kelly knew that was what he would say. Pa and Tim led the way carrying the luggage. Ma and Kelly followed with the picnic basket.

"Stay right behind me," Pa said over his shoulder. "I don't want to lose out on all that grub."

Inside the train a narrow aisle separated the two rows of small seats, upholstered in red mohair. Brass lamps with glass chimneys hung on the dark wood paneling. A black potbellied stove stood at the end of the car to warm passengers in the winter.

It was a narrow gauge train, which meant the rails were not as far apart as tracks are for standard gauge. The whole train, locomotive and all, seemed a scaled-down model, and Kelly never got over the idea this was a toy train that could take her to some make-believe land.

At last everyone was settled and the journey began. The engine continually burped black smoke, ashes, and sparks as it chugged along the line. The engineer stopped at the creek town sidings and wherever the miners appeared out of the brush, hat in hand, flagging down the train.

Picnic baskets were opened long before lunchtime. The aroma of deviled eggs and fried chicken hung heavy on the warm air. Passengers moved up and down the aisles and from car to car, talking, laughing, patting each other on the back. The Fourth of July celebration had begun.

As the train descended Pedro Dome to the valley below, the scenery slipped by unnoticed by the travelers. Spruce seedlings, colored bright green, roots firm in the mossy terrain, stood along the railroad tracks like a column of soldiers.

Birch, alder, and aspen trees, in full foliage, covered the gentle slopes of the nearby hills. The train rolled along across First Chance Creek, Engineer Creek, and Isabelle Creek to the train depot on Garden Island across the river from the main part of Fairbanks.

A hot sun bore down on the heads of the

townspeople crowded on the platform beside the terminal.

"There are the Bramsteads," Tim said, leaning out the window and waving.

"Where?" Kelly said, crowding beside him. Lucy and Evelyn were sitting in the wagon, dressed in cool white voile and with a ruffled parasol, held by Lucy, to protect them from the sun's glare.

"Don't they look pretty?" Kelly said, envy obvious in her voice. Her blue and white sailor dress, which she had suddenly outgrown this summer, would be a dowdy contrast. But then she added, "I don't see how they are going to race in those fancy clothes," flipping her braids back on her shoulders.

"I see Mike, too," Tim said.

"Is he with the Bramsteads?"

"No," Tim said, moving away from her. "I'm going to see if he'll save some seats for us at the grandstand." He hustled ahead while Kelly and Ma sought out the Bramsteads.

"Is that Mike over there?" Lucy wanted to know after they had exchanged greetings.

"Yes," Kelly said out loud. To herself she added, I bet Lucy knew Mike was there all the time. Hiding her feelings, Kelly climbed in the wagon.

Across the main road and situated in a grove of birch trees, Kelly could see the Catholic church with its slender spire. The shadows of the trees played on the grass and cast their shapes against the gleaming gray clapboard church.

Beyond was the hospital, a boxy two-story structure, run by the nuns in their black-and-white habits.

Warehouses built of wood occupied the space beside the train depot. Alongside the warehouses were Howard McGinney's livery stable and the J. P. Barrington machine shop, catering to the needs of the waterfront.

Docks had been built out into the silty Chena River to meet the stern-wheelers. These big steamships delivered the cargo that Fairbanks depended upon for its existence.

Except for the vegetables raised in the fields nearby and the wild game from the wooded hills, food, clothing, household, building, and mining supplies—all the necessities of life—came to this remote city from the "outside," as the townspeople said, meaning Seattle and points south.

In summer the boats were unloaded around the clock, as fast as the men could work. They had to bring in all the goods before the Tanana River and its tributary, the Chena, were clogged with ice sometime in early October.

Once the rivers were frozen, the only way in or out of Fairbanks was by the Winter Trail, a hazardous route 380 miles south to the ice-free port of Valdez. It was the same trail the Hansens had crossed when they first came to Alaska.

When winter settled in, the people of Fairbanks and the creek towns knew the meaning of isolation.

They were five days away from the nearest community of size, and this by fast dog team. They were a month away from Seattle. They were locked in, a mere speck in the vast Tanana Valley.

"Hurry, Tim," Kelly called. His boots made a clattering racket on the platform. Heads turned as he made his way to the wagon. He acknowledged the Bramstead girls' presence with a quick nod of his shaggy head, making sure he sat close to Kelly.

"I think we are ready now," Mr. Bramstead said.

Kelly nudged Tim. "Is Mike going to save seats for us?"

"He said he would."

"I hope he gets five right together," Evelyn purred beneath her parasol.

The wheels of the wagon rumbled over the wooden bridge spanning the Chena. This is going to be a good day, Kelly thought excitedly, stretching her neck to take in the flags dancing from the poles above the doorways, restaurants, dress shops, jewelry stores, saloons, grocery stores, and meat markets. Red, white, and blue bunting draped the riverfront grandstands where the crowd was already assembling for the parade.

"Look at all the people!" Kelly couldn't help shouting.

Evelyn pressed her handkerchief to her forehead and complained, "It's going to be so hot and crowded."

Mrs. Bramstead, a tall, long-necked lady of sedate manners, greeted the Hansens when they arrived at the house. After unloading the luggage, the two families walked the short blocks to town along the curve of the river, past log cabins set side by side on the dirt streets.

Some of the cabins, with pitched roofs, chinked logs, and white window sashes, were the same ones built by the first Fairbanks settlers in 1902. That was the year the Italian immigrant, Felix Pedro, discovered gold on the dome, a rise of land about twenty miles from where the city of Fairbanks now prospered.

About that same time Captain E. T. Barnette came steaming up the Chena in the stern-wheeler "La Velle Young," in search of a good place to establish a trading post. The merchant and the miner met. News of the gold strike spread. The stampede was on.

In ten short years the town, named for Senator Charles Fairbanks of Indiana, grew to a respectable community of several thousand people. Here stores, banks, churches, newspapers, a sawmill, library, brewery, and offices for doctors, lawyers, and dentists were built. Electricity, steam heat, and telephone service were provided to the downtown area. These people of the North could get things done.

Fairbanks was not an ordinary gold rush town. Nature had a hand in that. Gold did not pop out of the ground, it wasn't like the Klondike strike. The gold was not laced in the sand, ready for the taking, the way the stampeders found it in Nome.

The gold in Fairbanks was buried deep, under layers of frozen moss, mud, and gravel. It took back-breaking effort, time, and machinery to get the gold out. The get-rich-quick miners soon moved on. The true pioneers stayed to build a city that would outlast the other gold rush towns.

This pioneering spirit, this zeal to get things done, charged the atmosphere of Fairbanks. Here people stepped lively, kept their eyes straight on, and gave an honest welcome to friend and stranger alike.

Kelly was caught up in that spirit as she moved among the Fourth of July crowd. She had never smiled at so many people. If she wasn't careful, she just might begin to like Fairbanks.

Before the parade began, the mayor of the city spoke of freedom and independence and all things patriotic, while the people sat in the blazing sunlight on the grandstands. The flower-decked floats passed in review. H. R. Thomas's automobile had a place of importance in the parade, too. There weren't many of those newfangled gas buggies around town.

After the parade, Pa turned to Kelly and Tim. "Meet us at the Model Cafe at six o'clock. The Bramsteads are going to join us for dinner. You come, too, Mike," he offered, giving him a pat on the shoulder. That was Pa for you, never leaving anyone out.

"I'll try," Mike answered, hesitating. "I'm supposed to meet my pa around here somewhere." Everyone knew, including Mike, that his pa was at some saloon and would stay there until the holiday was over. Mr. Fessler had taken to drink after his wife died. Mike never spoke of it, not to a single person.

Mike and Tim led the way to Griffin Field, an open sandlot on the riverfront, where the races took place every year. The girls followed, two steps to one of the boys' long-legged strides.

Halfway there they stopped to buy peanuts and ice cream cones from the Italian man. Every Fourth of July he set up his stand. Somehow, nobody remembered seeing him the rest of the year.

"You gotta hava double dip," he said to all his customers. They did.

Before they reached the field, Lucy announced, "I'm not going to race this year." She continued to eat her ice cream cone, her pink tongue darting in and out. "I would ruin my dress," she explained.

Evelyn put in quickly, "I never race. I don't think it's becoming for a girl my age."

Kelly couldn't help but let a "Ha" escape her lips. She wasn't fooled by their silly excuses. The Bramstead girls didn't want to race because they knew they would lose. "I'm going to race and I'm going home with a pocketful of money," Kelly declared.

Such wholesale bragging was a dangerous

thing, Kelly knew. Statements like that had a way of turning on you and making you look foolish—it happened every time Kelly dared stick her neck out. She couldn't help it this time. She felt light and speedy—just like one of those rabbits Pa said she chased for breakfast.

When Kelly saw the girls lining up for the first race, she had serious misgivings. The tall ones, with sun-browned legs free from stockings, were the Hungarian girls from Olnes. To them, running was as effortless as breathing.

Mike saw Kelly's hesitation. "Go on," he urged. "You can beat them." His confidence filled her with courage.

The Bramstead girls, perching on a log, waved. "We're rooting for you, Kelly," Lucy called sweetly.

Kelly approached the starting line. The other girls moved to make space for her. None of them spoke. This was serious business. A ten dollar gold piece was the prize. Kelly longed to have it for her own.

"Winning isn't everything," Pa had said. Was it just this morning? It seemed years ago from this time and place. Winning *is* everything, Kelly thought. It is.

Kelly heard the starting shot. She sprang forward. Without looking to the left or the right, she pressed on, demanding more and more speed from her body. She could barely feel her feet touching the ground. Her arms pumped vigorously. The distance between her and the other girls lengthened. The shouts and cheers of the crowd became even louder as she crossed the finish line, her heart pounding inside her chest.

She had lived her entire thirteen years for this moment! Winning. The gold piece slipped into her hand was as smooth and warm as Pa's own palm.

After that, Kelly could not be stopped. She quickly became the crowd favorite. Friends and strangers alike cheered her on. She entered every race. She didn't win them all, but she quickly amassed a small fortune. Thirty-five dollars. She sweated victoriously and didn't care whether that was ladylike or not.

"What are you going to do with all that money?" Evelyn asked enviously. "I've never had that much money of my own ever."

"I have a special place for it," Kelly answered. She wasn't about to tell any more than that.

Tim and Mike had done all right, too. Their pockets were heavy with money.

"Come on," Mike said, "I'll buy everyone another ice cream cone."

They weren't hungry, or so they thought, as they joined the Hansens and the Bramsteads for dinner. But when the food came, sizzling steaks on thick platters, their appetites were miraculously revived straight through to dessert—cherry pie with ice cream.

After dinner, the two families walked back to

Griffin Field to watch the baseball game. Then they took a leisurely stroll along the river to watch the boat races. The Hansens and the Bramsteads took in everything. This kind of day would not come again for a whole year.

It would never be dark this night. Wasn't the sun shining at eleven o'clock proof enough? They had the fireworks display just the same. And for the climax, a man ascended before their eyes in a hot air balloon.

Walking back to the Bramsteads, the air was deliciously cool. The summer sun slipping behind the low, rounded hills to the west was like a stamp of approval on a day that Kelly would remember for a long time.

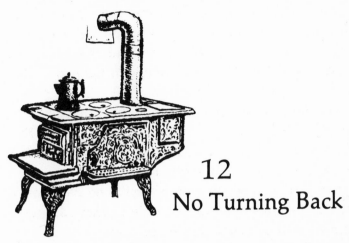

12
No Turning Back

It wasn't more than a minute ago, or so it seemed, that Kelly had tucked the pillow beneath her head and pulled the blankets under her chin.

But weren't those breakfast sounds she was hearing—cups clattering on saucers, voices raised in conversation, pans rattling on the stove? Bread toasting on wire racks and bacon popping in the skillet sent wake-up aromas into the Bramsteads' small back bedroom. It *was* morning.

Kelly slipped into yesterday's clothes and quickly ran her hands over her hair. She was the last one up. She hurried to the kitchen, where everyone was already seated at the large round table.

As she took her place, Kelly heard Mr. Bramstead saying, "If you people are really interested in a house to rent, there is one next door you might like to see."

"Oh, no," Kelly said. She clapped her hand over her mouth. The words were out before she could stop them. One quick glance, and Kelly knew her mother was not happy with her outburst.

Mrs. Bramstead cracked an egg in the pan as if nothing had happened.

The minister cleared his throat. He fingered the stem of his pipe. "I didn't mean to upset you, Kelly," he said. "I thought you were looking forward to moving into town."

Kelly tried to make herself smile, be pleasant, hide her feelings, but she couldn't. Instead, her mouth twisted into a painful expression.

Lucy and Evelyn watched expectantly. They felt Kelly would cry any minute.

Before Mr. Bramstead could offer words of consolation, Mrs. Hansen said, "We would like to see the house after breakfast." In her usual direct manner, Ma had settled the situation. The talk went on to speculation about the new dredge operation on the creeks.

Kelly didn't care to hear about that either. She poked at the food on her plate. The toast, bacon, and eggs that had piqued her appetite a few minutes ago seemed like sand in her mouth.

Breakfast came to an end. Kelly's egg was a cold, sticky glob on her plate. No one told her to eat.

"You folks go ahead and look at the house," Mrs. Bramstead said, getting up from the table. "Lucy and Evelyn will do the dishes."

154

Ma was already scraping the plates. "I would be happy to help," she said.

"Oh, no, I wouldn't hear of it," Mrs. Bramstead answered. "I know you have a lot to do before you catch the train this afternoon."

The minister went to the kitchen cupboard. "I'll get the keys. Yes, here they are. The house belongs to some members of our congregation who had to move back to Oregon. They left some furniture." He directed an encouraging smile towards Kelly. "I think you will like the house."

Kelly took her plate to the sink. If she stalled long enough, maybe they would go without her.

"You can come with us now," Ma said in her I-mean-business voice. It was not an invitation. It was a command.

Kelly had the urge to slam the kitchen door behind her. Instead, she swallowed the hard lump in her throat and followed her family.

Not a leaf stirred on the raspberry bushes growing along the slat fence separating the two houses. The heat was coming down hard like a sledgehammer. Another scorcher.

Wild iris in a shaggy green clump, brown around the edges from lack of water, grew in the front yard. A wooden sidewalk, wider than most, led to the screened front porch.

The house, long and narrow, reminded Kelly of a boxcar on a train. It's about as colorful, too, she thought, taking in the unstained logs and raw window trim. The front part of the house was built of logs. There was a frame addition at the back attached to the house by a shed with a sloping roof.

"The house needs some fixing up," Mr. Bramstead was saying as he fumbled with the lock. "No one has lived here since winter." He opened the door and they were met by a wave of warm, musty air.

The Hansens stepped over the doorsill. Dust stood thick on the tabletops. The windowsills were gray with it. A fly buzzed drunkenly at the smudged windowpanes.

Ma ran her finger along the sill. "There is as much dust here as in Gold City."

"Front Street is well traveled," the minister remarked.

The living room was small, Kelly noticed. It's even smaller than our living room at home in Gold City, she thought. Only dim light entered the room through the north window shaded by the front porch. There was a narrow walk-through dining room and an equally small bedroom, barely big enough for a double bed and dresser.

At the back, in the frame addition, was the kitchen and an eating area. Nobody could call it a dining room. The black wood stove, wedged in one corner, dominated the room. A wall-hung sink had a bucket under it to catch the water. There was no running water, no sewer lines in this part of town. The Hansens would be no better off than in Gold City.

Corner windows, with a wooden table beneath them, let plenty of light into the room. Off the kitchen was the pantry with shelves from floor to ceiling.

Kelly took in the surroundings with growing dismay. It was an ugly house without a speck of charm. The walls were covered with spotted paper. In each room a bare light bulb hung from the ceiling by a cord.

"Where would I sleep?" Kelly asked. There was only one bedroom.

"In the living room on a daybed, I suppose," Ma said. She didn't like that idea any better than Kelly.

It is bad enough leaving Gold City, Kelly thought, but not having a room of my own makes it even worse.

"We all have to make sacrifices," Pa reminded her.

She knew Pa was right, but why did her sacrifices always seem bigger than anyone else's?

"We haven't decided to take the house yet," Ma reminded her.

Kelly knew by the calculating look in Ma's eye that she was mentally papering the walls, putting down new rugs, moving in her own furniture, cleaning the windows, and hanging new curtains.

Ma, surveying the dining room with a critical eye, turned to Pa, "It wouldn't be so bad after we got our own things in here." She *was* remodeling the place, just as Kelly had suspected.

In the small bedroom closet Tim found a ladder that led to the attic. "Hey, Pa," his voice was muffled, "I can sleep up here."

They trooped into the tiny closet. Pa craned his neck trying to see where Tim had disappeared. "Watch your step up there, son," Pa said.

"Kelly, come on up," Tim called.

She climbed the narrow ladder to the attic. Above her the rafters stuck out like the ribs of a prehistoric monster. At the far end a dust-spotted window let in a stingy amount of sunlight. Boxes, a broken chair, stacks of old magazines, fuzzy with dust, were pushed against the eaves.

"Watch your head," Tim cautioned.

Kelly ducked just in time. There was no flooring. She carefully placed her feet on the cross-beams. One false move and she would be through the plaster ceiling of the floor below.

"You can't sleep up here. It's awful."

"It will be all right once I fix it up."

"The whole house is awful."

"It wouldn't matter what kind of a house it was —you wouldn't like it," Tim said. "You just don't want to leave Gold City, that's all."

Tim was like Pa. He could sum things up in one neat package. He paused, halfway down the ladder. "Have you ever thought how Pa feels about giving up the store or how Ma likes moving into a smaller house? It won't be easy for them either, but they will do it if it means a better life for all of us."

Kelly sat on a box of books. Why am I always wrong and everybody else is always right? she wondered. She propped her head in her hand. I would like to be miserable just once without someone telling me why I shouldn't be.

She shifted uncomfortably. If only I could look at things from the outside in, she thought, instead of from the inside out where everything starts with me.

She had to admit that the move into Fairbanks would mean an adjustment for the whole family. She slowly concluded, maybe it wasn't that her adjustment would be bigger, but just that she was resisting harder. She would think about that, she promised herself. She wasn't going to make any instant about-face. These things take time.

She stood up suddenly. "Owwww!" she yelped, rubbing her head where she hit it on the rafters.

"What's wrong?" Pa called from below.

"I bumped my head."

"Come down before anything else happens," Pa said. "We are ready to leave."

Kelly walked through the empty house. Dust twirled in the shafts of sunlight streaking through the windows. She had a feeling she would return here. She caught up with Pa and grabbed his hand. His eyes said everything will be all right. Just wait and see.

There was time for shopping before boarding the train. The Hansens walked to town. The Bram-

159

steads would meet them later at the depot with their luggage.

Tim and Pa went on business of their own, while Kelly and Ma went shopping up and down Second Avenue and along Cushman Street. Well-stocked store windows offered a tantalizing array of merchandise, from imported candies and writing paper to shiny black dancing slippers with silver buckles. Kelly held five dollars of her prize money tied in a handkerchief. Pa had the rest safe inside his vest pocket.

Whenever Ma admired a flowered hat or knit shawl in a store window, Kelly wanted to rush in and buy it for her.

"No," Ma said, "you save your money."

There is nothing to save it for, Kelly said to herself. Even if I spent the whole thirty-five dollars in one day, it wouldn't matter. Why save it? It won't help us stay in Gold City. She had faced that fact earlier that day, looking at the new house.

"Why don't you buy some material and I will make you a dress for school?" Ma suggested. They were standing in the dry goods section at the Katherine Mills store. Bolts of rich fabrics towered above them on the shelves.

"I have some new chambray in a beautiful dark blue," the clerk said helpfully. "It would go so nicely with your blue eyes."

They decided on the blue chambray with white lace and black grosgrain ribbon to trim the collars

160

and cuffs. "I bought it with my own money," Kelly thought, tucking the package under her arm. There was a feeling of independence, of growing up in that.

At the depot a tired, subdued collection of people waited to board the train home. Women in rumpled dresses held sleeping babies. Men gathered the luggage with an effort. The holiday was over.

Ma and Kelly met Pa and Tim at the station. In a few minutes the Bramsteads arrived with the Hansens' luggage. Ma and Pa thanked the minister and his wife for their hospitality and promised to let them know their decision on the new house.

Good-byes were said as the Hansens boarded the train. The cars were not as crowded as they had been yesterday. Many families stayed an extra day in Fairbanks. The Hansens could pick and choose the seats they preferred. People sat apart from each other, too tired to talk.

Gray clouds pushed across the sky, blotting out the sun, leaving a wan shadowless light. The air coming in through the train windows was cool.

Kelly settled comfortably next to an open window. She leaned her head on the cushioned seat while the train made its grinding and squealing getting-started noises. Soon the train picked up speed as it traveled into the misty blue-green countryside.

13
Why Did It Happen, Harry?

It was all out in the open now. One late July evening when Kelly was with Pa at the store, he told her they had made the decision. The family would leave Gold City.

Now all the things she had feared were coming true. Pa was selling the store. The Hansens were moving to Fairbanks. They would live next door to the Bramsteads. Kelly would go to the big school in town.

Later that week, when Kelly went to the mine and put her hand on the rocker, the joy she had known earlier was gone. Gold mining was hard work now. Mighty hard work. Her heart wasn't in it. There was no driving need for the gold. She had no cause to fight for. Gold mining for gold itself was not enough for her. She could never save the store.

Kelly felt helpless in the face of the changes taking place around her. Each day drifted by like a leaf moving across a pond.

162

The last week in July the word spread through Gold City with the suddenness of a flash flood—the berries in the bogs south of town were ripe.

The sun had done its work well. The bushes were blue with berries—round, plump berries just waiting to fall into the buckets.

Kelly gladly gave up gold mining this day to go berrying with Ma. The first trip was always the best of the season.

"We will stop and see if the Bonovich children would like to come with us," Ma said as she tied a red bandana around her head.

Kelly packed their lunch in the tin berry buckets. "We have enough sandwiches for Hilda and Einar if they do come," she said.

They splashed citronella on their arms and necks to ward off the mosquitoes nesting in the damp bogs. When Kelly got desperate, she put newspaper inside her long cotton stockings to protect her legs from the bugs. But that was a last resort. She certainly wasn't going to walk down the road like that.

Ma folded a sweater over her arm. "I don't think I'll need this sweater," she said, gathering the berry buckets, "but I'll take it along just in case."

The sun was warm, not hot. The air was freshly washed by an early morning rain. Small puddles of rainwater collected in the pockets of the road and reflected patches of sky and scraps of clouds.

"Pa is going to come get us at three o'clock,"

Ma said. "That should give us plenty of time to pick."

Kelly nodded. Her thoughts were busy with the blueberry desserts that were in the offing—pies, dumplings, muffins. Sauce and syrup for shortcake and pancakes. Berrying in summer made the season worthwhile. At least that hasn't changed, Kelly thought.

During the two years Mrs. Bonovich had lived in Gold City, she made little attempt to mix with the wives of the miners. She held herself apart from others, putting on airs of superiority. The women thought her rude and lacking in common courtesies.

Mrs. Bonovich with her sharp tongue and aggressive manner would never be one of them. She isolated her family from the people of Gold City. She fought the environment instead of learning to live with it. She tried to make her life the same as it had been in Europe. She shrugged off advice on how to cope with the new life in Alaska—the weather, dressing properly, gardening, using wild meat, and planning ahead for the seasons.

If anyone had reached a small measure of understanding with Mrs. Bonovich, it was Ma. She had cut through the woman's pretenses without offending her.

Ma didn't go often to the Bonovich cabin, but when she did go, she usually accomplished her purpose. As she did this day.

Hilda and Einar stayed close to Kelly and Ma

on the way to the berry patch. Mrs. Bonovich's constant warnings about the wild animals roaming the hills had frightened them both. The children never dared venture beyond the fence railings of their yard. Today they felt brave taking on this adventure with the Hansens.

Ma took this berry picking business seriously. She attacked the bushes the way a general assaults the enemy. Once the battleground was established, Ma picked fiercely until the bushes were bare. "No lollygagging," was her theme. "You girls watch Einar," she said.

"We will," they answered.

"I be good," Einar said impulsively. He was an obedient child whose curiosity had been dulled by his mother's constant scolding. It was easy to forget he was there.

Hilda and Kelly found a good patch where the berries hung in heavy clusters on the low, scrubby bushes. At first they ate more than they put in their buckets, stuffing the warm, sweet berries in their mouths until their teeth turned blue.

There was an unannounced competition between Kelly and Hilda to see who could fill her bucket first. Kelly squatted down, placed the bucket close to her knees and began pulling the berries off the bushes with both hands. They fell into the pail with a faint plunk-plunk sound. Hilda copied Kelly's every move. Hilda's brown fingers, nimble and quick, fluttered over the bushes like birds' wings.

There is a certain stillness in a berry patch, especially when the day is bright and a stiff breeze sets only the topmost leaves to twirling on the far-away birch and aspen. It is the sound of dry twigs snapping underfoot, the buzz of insects zipping through the air, the clink-clinking of berry buckets. Kelly felt in tune with the outdoor music. The berries rained thick and fast into her pail.

From her patch Kelly could see Einar's sturdy, round figure bent over the bushes a few feet away.

"How are you doing, Einar?" she called.

"I do good," he answered. "Look." He held up his bucket.

Kelly couldn't see inside, but she suspected by his berry-smeared face that he was eating more fruit than he was putting in his bucket.

Hilda stayed close to Kelly, close enough to reach out and touch her if need be. When Kelly moved, Hilda jumped up to follow.

It was hard for Kelly to understand Hilda's fear. The trees on the wooded hillsides, the birds that nested there, the animals that walked the paths to the creeks, the flowers that bloomed among the rocks, were as familiar to Kelly as her own hands and face.

"You do not have to be afraid here," Kelly tried to tell her friend.

"I don't want to be alone out here," Hilda protested. "Mama never lets me. Never alone outdoors. She always tells me that." Thick lashes veiled her solemn eyes. "Many dangers everywhere." She gestured with her short, dark hands, taking in the wide expanse of the berry patch.

"I've lived here all my life," Kelly said, "and I have never been harmed." The security and freedom, the sense of belonging in Gold City, was as much a part of Kelly as her own breathing. She wanted to share that feeling with Hilda.

Hilda lifted her head in a gesture she had learned from her mother. "We come from big city. My father was important businessman. We do not belong in wild country like this. We not like it here."

Kelly was taken back by Hilda's tone. She hadn't suspected that behind that quiet face with the hesitant smile there was such a proud spirit.

"We are not like other people. We are different." The way Hilda said it, Kelly knew she meant "We are better."

Kelly let the argument drop. There was no use in arguing about it. She had tried to help Hilda, but Hilda didn't want to be helped. Why must people keep their minds closed so tight? Kelly wondered.

It was hard to tell how much time had passed. The sun, high in the sky, seemed nailed to the same spot. Yet an inner sense told Kelly that something was different.

Hilda was so close to Kelly that she could see the beads of perspiration on her upper lip. Where was Einar? She looked over to the bushes where she had seen him last. The patch was abandoned, and Einar was nowhere in sight.

"Hilda," Kelly said, trying to make her voice sound natural, "do you see Einar anywhere?"

Hilda's dark head went up suddenly. She scanned the field, the blackish-green leaves glinted like sun on water. Hilda shaded her eyes, squinting nervously. "He is gone," she said fearfully.

"Ma!" Kelly yelled. "Ma!"

No answer. A threatening silence hung over the berry patch. Kelly could feel Hilda's fear. She herself was touched by it. Somehow they had moved away from the main patch. Had Einar followed Ma or had he gone off on his own?

Kelly picked up her bucket. "Come on, Hilda," she said. "Let's find Ma. Einar is probably with her."

Tears flooded Hilda's eyes. "Some animal eat him, poor baby," she said. "What will Mama say?"

Kelly didn't want to think about Mrs. Bonovich right now. "Oh, Einar is probably with Ma." Kelly wished she felt as confident as her voice sounded. "Come on, follow me."

In blueberry country everything looks the same —miles and miles of sameness. The large patches of berries are surrounded by growths of stunted spruce and dwarf birch. There are no landmarks to set one acre apart from another. The rolling fields flow along over gulches that are carbon copies of each other.

Walking in blueberry country is not easy either. The bog is full of muskeg, hummocks of wild grass in a clump of permanently frozen dirt, surrounded by pools of water. Kelly was never sure whether it was better to leap from one grassy top to another or wade through the swamp water.

"I don't think we are very far from where we left Ma," Kelly said, trying to reassure Hilda.

"You mean we are *lost?*" Tears, the biggest Kelly had ever seen, rolled down Hilda's cheeks.

"No, we are not lost," Kelly said, a bit too loudly to be convincing. "If we can find the thicket of trees where we left our lunch, we will be all right. Ma can't be far from there."

"I should have stayed home. I should have stayed home," Hilda wailed. Her stockings were wet above her knees. Locks of damp, dark hair fell over her face.

At any moment Kelly expected to see Ma's red bandana poking above the bushes and to hear her reassuring voice. Kelly looked and listened in vain. They kept walking. Kelly was not even sure now they were going in the right direction. The ground had become smoother, drier underfoot.

"This doesn't look right at all," Hilda said, stopping to survey the countryside. "We have walked too far."

She was right. Kelly felt helpless. This had never happened to her before. Lost in the blueberry bogs. She wanted to blame it on Hilda's foolish fears. Somehow she thought that was the reason for the whole mess.

Hilda started to cry again. "Oh, where is Einar? I hate this place. I hate it." She sat on the ground, burying her head in her hands.

"It's no help at all for you to cry, Hilda," Kelly said without sympathy. "We have to keep walking." She started on, and Hilda followed.

The mosquitoes were on them, biting knuckles and wrists, forehead and eyebrows, scalp and neck. The sun blazed unmercifully. Kelly lifted her hair off her neck and her skin was damp with perspiration.

Somewhere along the line the berries had spilled out of Kelly's bucket. It was only half full now. She felt the panic rise in her throat. All we need now is some prowling animal, Kelly thought, and Hilda will be hysterical. The girl was already whimpering with each step.

Kelly feared they were going around in circles. Usually she could depend on her sense of direction to get her out of such predicaments. Where was that sense now?

Kelly stopped. She thought she heard a voice.

"What's wrong?" Hilda sniffed.

"Shhh." Kelly strained hard to hear. "Ma," she yelled. "Maaa!"

A faint "Yoo-hoo," came across the bogs.

In the distance Kelly could see the red bandana. It was the loveliest sight Kelly had ever seen. Ma was waving. "Over here," she called.

Suddenly the fear vanished—as quickly as mist vanishes in the sun. Just like that. Kelly grabbed Hilda's hand. They ran calling, "Is Einar with you?"

"Yes," came the welcoming answer. "He is right here."

"Thank goodness," Kelly said, falling at Ma's feet. "We were so worried." She could admit that now.

"Ya, ya," was all Hilda could say as she hugged her brother.

"I found the best patch," Ma said, unaware of the fear the girls had felt. "Look." Her bucket was overflowing with berries as big as marbles. She picked "clean" and had taught Kelly to do the same. They rarely had twigs and leaves in their pails.

"When we eat?" Einar said when Hilda finally let him go.

Everyone laughed. They were all thinking about lunch, too.

"Right now," Ma answered. She went ahead with the berry buckets. Kelly carried Einar piggyback over the muskeg. She didn't let Ma out of her sight.

The moose meat sandwiches were unwrapped and quickly eaten. The cold boiled potatoes sprinkled with salt tasted better eaten outdoors than they ever did at the kitchen table. The jar of lemonade, a little warm from sitting in the sun, was drained to the last drop. Still there was room for them to eat loaf cake, every crumb licked away.

Stomachs full, they stretched out on the ground, letting the sun cover them with its warmth. The air was heavy with the scent of grasses growing in wet places, of wildflowers and weeds crushed underfoot. They could relax like this forever, except the mosquitoes wouldn't let them. Slap! Slap! There was no peace.

"Back to the berry bushes," Ma said, jumping up with her energy quickly renewed. "We might as well fight the bugs while we pick berries."

They set out with pails banging against their legs. This time they stayed within sight of each other. Every now and then Ma's "Yoo-hoo" was heard across the berry patch. Three "Yoo-hoo's" came back in reply.

By three o'clock the berry picking came to a stop. Feet dragging, backs aching from a day of bending over berry bushes, Hilda and Kelly made their way back to the picnic spot. Ma and Einar soon joined them.

"We did a good stroke of business today," Ma said, counting the filled-to-the-brim buckets. "Let's start carrying the berries to the road so we are ready when Pa comes."

They walked single file across the bogs. A pile of whipped clouds, fringed with yellow light, moved across the sun. The thing Kelly wanted most to do when she got home was put her hot, mosquito-bitten feet into the cold water of Crooked Creek.

Kelly was the first one to spot the tail of dust in

the distance, funneling up from the road. "Someone is coming," she said. Whoever it was had to be traveling fast to kick up that much dust. "It's Pa!" Kelly shouted. "It's Pa!"

"Something must be wrong," Ma said. "He never drives that fast."

Hilda started crying. "I want to go home." Einar huddled close to her skirt.

A heavy mantle of dust swept over them as Pa pulled to an abrupt halt. Dolly and Bravo were in a sweat. "We have to hurry," Pa said, jumping down from the wagon to load the berries.

"What is wrong?" Ma asked anxiously.

"It's a fire," Pa said. "I have to get back to help."

"Where did it start?" Ma asked, lifting Einar into the back to the wagon. Kelly and Hilda jumped in beside him.

Kelly echoed, "Where?"

"At Harry Mudge's cabin," Pa said, turning the wagon toward town.

"At Harry's place?" Kelly cried. "Oh, Pa! What about Harry? Is he all right?"

"Yes," Pa answered. "Harry's safe. The men are trying to save the cabin and keep the fire from spreading to the woods."

"How did it happen?" Ma asked. She held on to the wagon seat to keep from being pitched out because Pa traveled the rutted road at a fast clip.

"They aren't sure," Pa yelled over the rattling

of the wagon. "They think it got started in a pile of sawdust. It's burning mighty fast."

Fire was a constant threat in the creek towns. There was no equipment and little water to fight the blaze. The men, armed with axes and shovels, would cut a fire line around the blaze to contain it. If a wind started up carrying the sparks across the line, the fire could rage out of control, consuming the hillsides, destroying birds and animals, wiping out towns in a matter of hours. All that remained would be a heap of ashes watched over by skeleton trees, charred black.

Pa slapped the reins over the horses' backs harder than he ever did. The wagon shuddered. "Watch the berry buckets," Ma said over her shoulder.

Mrs. Bonovich was waiting by the side of the road. She scooped Einar out of the wagon even before it came to a stop. "Look that sky," she yelled. "We will all burn up!" The air was white with smoke, littered with flying ash.

Hilda jumped down and Kelly handed her two berry buckets. "Good-bye," Hilda said, as if they would never see each other again.

Won't she ever grow up, Kelly thought, and learn to take things as they come? But it's always easier to tell someone else how to act, she reminded herself. I hope I don't act as stubborn as Hilda does when I get to Fairbanks.

Pa stopped at the house to let Ma off. "Kelly,

don't go near the fire," Ma said. "You stay in the wagon."

Kelly nodded. She climbed into the wagon seat with Pa and they started off for Harry's cabin. Women and children, lining the road, stepped back as the wagon approached. Smoke billowed above the treetops. The smell of burning wood carried for miles.

As they neared Harry's place Kelly could see the flames licking skyward. The sound of wood cracking and popping in the fire was as loud as gunshots. Wagons, pulled off the road at haphazard angles, added to the confusion. Horses whinnied frantically.

Pa pulled off the road until the wagon was tipping halfway into the ditch. "You stay here, Kelly," he said, jumping down and running toward the fire.

Kelly waited until Pa was out of sight. Then she slipped to the ground and headed straight for Harry's cabin. She had to know whether Harry was safe. She had to help.

The tall trees along the driveway were shrouded in ghostly veils of smoke. Kelly quickened her pace. The smoke burned her lungs. She held her hand across her mouth. Above the noise of the fire, the men's voices rang out, "More water! More water!"

It was hopeless. They could never save the cabin—the men weren't even trying. The interior of the cabin was a rolling boil of flames.

The men, bare backs glistening with sweat, dug with their shovels to contain the fire. A trench helped prevent the flames from spreading to the heavily wooded section nearby. Water hauled in by the barrel was poured on the ground along the trench.

Kelly picked up a shovel and began throwing dirt on the fire. The heat was intense. In an instant her eyelashes and hair were singed.

"Here. Let me do that."

It was Mike. His soot-smudged face was that of a stranger. He took the shovel from her. She wanted to help, but she couldn't. The heat drove her from his side.

"Stand back! Stand back!" the men shouted.

As the warning rang out the roof of the cabin, Harry's wonderful sod roof where the wild grasses grew went crashing to the ground. A shower of sparks flew high and wide.

Kelly turned away. She couldn't watch. Through the smoke she could see Harry's staunch and sturdy figure over by the garden. He was look-ing at the patch of potatoes that still grew in the gloomy, smoky afternoon light. Kelly grabbed his arm and hugged it to her. She smelled the smoke on his clothes.

"How is my girl?" It was Harry's same dear, familiar voice, as if nothing had happened at all.

"Harry, this is awful." Tears choked in Kelly's throat. "Why did it have to happen to you?"

He looked at her with those wonderful eyes that had seen so much of life. "Would you have it happen to someone else?"

"No, of course not," Kelly said, squeezing his arm. "I wouldn't have it happen at all."

Harry mopped his forehead with his handkerchief, gray after too many washings in cold water. "But it did happen," he said, turning to look at the remains of his cabin and his possessions. "It did happen," he said as if he still didn't quite believe it himself.

"Kelly," Pa called, spotting her across the yard. "I told you to stay in the wagon." He was angry. "This is no place for you. You start walking home. Straight home," he added for emphasis.

"I will, Pa," she said. She stood on tiptoe and kissed Harry on the cheek where his beard grew soft and silky. She turned and ran before he could see the tears in her eyes.

It wasn't until Kelly was almost home that she thought of it. Her gold, the gold she had mined all summer, had burned up in Harry's cabin. He had hidden it so carefully under the floor boards that were now smoldering coals.

She felt guilty thinking about her loss—it was small compared to Harry's—but it seemed the hardest and cruelest blow to all her efforts that summer.

14
Gold Nuggets

The days of August are deceiving. The sun rises high and bright in a pure, cloudless sky, stamping sharp shadows of trees on tar paper roofs and outlines of buildings against damp fields of grass. But there is no warmth in this flood of sunlight.

Kelly slipped her hands inside the sleeves of her sweater. Her fingertips were freezing, but she didn't care. She continued walking.

The air tingled with a new freshness, starched by the morning frost. Kelly skipped over the small puddles ringed with ice.

She had awakened early this morning, long before Pa's alarm rang. She was wide awake and felt a strong urge to get dressed and go out walking while she could have Gold City to herself.

As she passed each cabin and the sleeping people within, Kelly said good-bye to them in her own silent way. When I am a very old person, she thought, I will still remember these cabins with their flower boxes of red and yellow nasturtiums, and the woods of pointed spruce.

Even without consciously thinking about it, Kelly knew where she was going. She was propelled forward by some unknown force along the path past the splashing creek and up the slope to the summit where she had dug crocus—was it only five months ago? It seemed longer—and shorter, too. How could it be both? she wondered. It all depends upon how you look at it, she reasoned.

Splatterings of honey-colored leaves gleamed among the green where the frost had touched the birch and aspen trees. Kelly's feet swished through a pile of leaves fallen on the path like so many gold coins. As she made her way to the top, the cranberry bushes took on a deep ruby red glow, spreading before her like a flame.

Kelly looked carefully among the rocks. There was no evidence that she had dug crocus on this summit. It disappointed her that there was no sign that she had been there.

Below her the sun shone full of yellow brightness on Gold City, a toy town from here. Along Crooked Creek, not far from Pa's store, newly felled trees scarred the landscape. On that land the gold dredging company would erect bunkhouses and a dining hall. There the huge piece of machinery would eat up the land, squealing and whining.

Kelly turned away. The changes were galloping past her like a runaway team. I don't want to be left behind, Kelly thought. She paused a minute on her way down the trail. Wasn't that what Mr. Winslow had said would happen? Maybe I am growing up after all, she thought.

Since the fire, Kelly had not been able to make herself go to Harry's place, but today was a different day. She felt drawn there as she had felt drawn to the summit.

She walked faster, anxious now to reach her destination. Spruce cones crackled beneath her boots, alerting the lively tan squirrels that she was approaching.

Kelly's stomach grumbled noisily, reminding her that she had not eaten yet today. She hoped Harry would be at his place with some good grub cooking.

A plume of gray smoke rose from the campfire. Kelly could see Harry, pancake turner in hand, standing by a small canvas tent pitched in front of the garden. A short distance away Kelly saw the heap of charred timbers and ashes—all that was left of Harry's cabin.

"Harry," she called, "am I in time for breakfast?"

"How many sourdough pancakes can you eat?" he hollered.

"At least two hundred."

"What brings you out so early in the morning?" he asked as she neared.

"I just had to look at things."

He knew what she meant. She never had to explain things to Harry. They hadn't talked much about her leaving Gold City. He was like that, letting her work things out on her own, never preaching like some grown-ups did.

They sat side by side on upturned logs in front of the fire, eating pancakes drenched in syrup. Harry talked about rebuilding his cabin, getting it ready before winter.

"There is a lot of work to be done," he said, and the twinkle was back in his eye. "Mike is going to help me until he leaves."

"Leaves!" Kelly said, lifting her face to his. "Where is Mike going?"

"I thought you knew," Harry went on calmly. "He is going to live with his aunt in Fairbanks this winter."

The news hit her like a dash of cold water in the face. Mike—going to Fairbanks. She almost laughed out loud at the trick circumstances had played on her.

Here she had spent the whole summer working to stay in Gold City. She tried to keep around her all the people she knew and loved. She wanted to keep things exactly the way they had always been, when all the time everything was slipping out of her reach.

"That means we will go to school together," Kelly said.

"Yup, it sure does," Harry agreed, fiddling with the fire.

"That won't be so bad then," Kelly said, "at least I will know one person in school."

"What about those cute Bramstead girls?" Harry was teasing and she knew it.

"I didn't forget them, I was just ignoring them for the time being."

Harry chuckled. "You'll do all right in Fairbanks. Yes, sir, you'll do all right."

Before Kelly left she washed the two tin plates, cups, and silverware in a pan of creek water warmed over the campfire.

When Kelly got home, Ma was at the packing again. She had started three days ago. The order and harmony of the rooms, with chairs, tables, lamps, and rugs always in their proper places, disappeared the day the packing boxes were brought in.

Books were off bookshelves, leaving dusty lines where they had stood. Curtains were off windows, revealing sills with cracked paint. The rugs were up, exposing the rough floorboards.

Dresser drawers stood half open. The winter clothes were packed for town. The summer clothes were stored in closets, ready for the family's return next summer.

Pa had promised that they would come back for a few weeks after school was out. There is that to look forward to, Kelly thought as she wandered from room to room. Pa's promise reassured her like a light at the far end of a dark tunnel.

"Where have you been?" Ma asked, looking up

from her task. She was taking pictures off the living room walls, dusting them and packing them with the linens. The pictures left blank white squares against the dust-darkened burlap.

The house will never, never be the same, Kelly thought before she answered Ma. "I went for a walk. Harry invited me to stop for pancakes," she said, anticipating that Ma would ask her whether she had eaten. "Where is Tim? I thought he was supposed to help pack."

"They want him to work at the mine until we leave," Ma answered.

He always gets out of the housework, Kelly thought. You'd think he could at least help pack since he's the one so anxious to go to Fairbanks. She didn't air those thoughts with Ma. That would only bring on an argument she could never win.

"What do you want me to do?" Kelly asked, more out of duty than desire.

Ma hesitated. "There is so much sorting I have to do," she said, brushing a wisp of hair off her forehead. "Why don't you work in the garden? We have to get all those vegetables in before we leave."

"All right," Kelly said without enthusiasm. She purposely let the screen door bang behind her.

Once she got into the job it wasn't so bad. Down on her hands and knees in the garden Kelly remembered the early summer days she had worked putting the seeds in the ground. Now she was taking out vegetables. There was some satisfaction in that, as if everything was completing an important cycle in her life.

Kelly sat back on her heels. She shook the dirt off a carrot and wiped it on the underside of her skirt. She chewed the crisp carrot thoughtfully.

It is really final now. We are leaving. We are leaving. Somehow she didn't feel as depressed as she had expected to be. I do feel sad about it, she argued with herself, but it doesn't hurt as much as I thought it would.

She probed her feelings the way one wiggles a loose tooth, to see what it takes to make it hurt.

For Kelly there was no sharp pain, just a small ache.

But the hardest part of moving was the day Kelly helped Pa in the store for the last time. Every customer that came in shook Pa's hand and said, "Sure going to miss you," or "Wish you didn't have to leave," or "Gold City won't be the same without you." Things like that.

There were those who slipped Pa money on their accounts with the promise to send him more money when they could.

Kelly had never been so proud of her father before. He seemed to grow taller before her eyes. She basked in the praise the people had for him. The bell over the door never stopped ringing.

When Kelly saw Mrs. Turnbarge enter, she got ready for the worst. Here is a way to ruin the day, she thought, trying to make herself invisible behind a table of overalls. By now, Kelly knew Mrs. Turn-barge's bill had been paid. But she didn't wish to recall that long-ago episode as storekeeper.

"Mr. Hansen," the woman's boisterous voice rang with false gaiety, "I shall miss you, I truly shall." She clasped his hand as if they were the best of friends.

"It's been a pleasure serving you," Pa said gallantly. He could always rise to the occasion.

"And the family," Mrs. Turnbarge said, "how do they feel about leaving?"

"They are doing fine, just fine," Pa said, evading the question.

Kelly made her way to the back door. She was getting out while it was safe. She could feel the tears starting in her eyes. Mrs. Turnbarge knew every-body's weak spot.

The ragged bushes beside the store were hung with yellow leaves. There was a musty heaviness in the air that was not unpleasant, like ripe fruit in a paper bag.

The sight of a familiar horse and wagon hitched in front of the house sent Kelly bursting into the liv-ing room. "Ma," she cried, "why didn't you tell me Harry was here?" She threw herself into Harry's arms before she realized Mike was there, too. Kelly pulled back, suddenly embarrassed. Her face flamed red. She didn't want Mike to see her act that way.

"They just got here," Ma said. "I'll get the coffee."

186

Kelly stood awkwardly. There was no place for her to sit. Packing boxes still littered the living room. Kelly was almost glad they were leaving tomorrow morning, if only to get away from the mess.

"We have something for you, Kelly," Harry said, breaking the silence. He pulled a poke of gold out of his pocket and handed it to her.

Kelly held her hands clenched tightly behind her. "What is it?" she asked hesitantly.

"Take it and see," Mike said, anxious that she should get on with it. This summer his voice had deepened, like Tim's. His face had matured. There was a tanned and ruddy glow to his skin.

Kelly held the moosehide pouch in her hand. "It's heavy," she said. Her blue eyes searched Harry's face for a clue. She was afraid to hope. It couldn't be, it couldn't be, she thought quickly as she poured the contents in her hand.

Gold nuggets! The very same nuggets she had panned at the mine. She could tell by their shape and size. "My gold!" she said, still not believing it. "They are my nuggets." She had never mentioned the nuggets to Harry, but she had thought about them often enough these past weeks. "How did you find them?" she asked.

"I put Mike to work panning the ashes where I thought the floorboards should be."

"Oh," Kelly said, hugging Harry and not feeling the least bit shy, "I never thought I'd get them back."

"I don't think I found all the gold dust," Mike said, "but it wasn't hard getting the big pieces."

Kelly cleared a space on top of a box and spread out the nuggets. She knew exactly what she was going to do with the gold now. It was as if it was meant to be from the start.

"What have we here?" Ma asked as she came sailing into the room. In one hand she carried the blue enamel pot steaming with freshly brewed coffee, in the other, a plate of store-bought cookies.

Kelly scooped the nuggets into the poke. "It is my pay for the work I did at the mine," Kelly said. She didn't have to explain any more to Ma. She knew all along what Kelly had been doing.

"I hear you are going to live in Fairbanks this winter," Ma said to Mike.

"Yes, ma'am."

"I hope you come to see us often. We are going to miss our Gold City friends. That means you too, Harry," Ma said, her eyes shiny bright. She handed Harry a cup of coffee. Her lips struggled with a smile. "It's going to be hard to leave."

Kelly had never heard Ma say that before. Never a word about how she felt. We all have our own hurts, Kelly realized. She cleared a chair for Ma. "Sit here," Kelly said. She had never felt closer to Ma than she did right then.

After Mike and Harry left, Kelly and Ma sat in the living room, the packing boxes looming around them, empty coffee cups on the floor.

The afternoon sunlight, mellowed by the changing season, slanted through the curtainless windows. In the kitchen the stove ticked contentedly, sending warmth throughout the house.

"Tomorrow at this time we will be on the train," Kelly said. It was hard to believe they could be ready and on their way by then. It seemed they would go on packing forever and ever and never quite leave.

"After all these years, it is hard to leave," Ma said wistfully. "You and Tim were raised here. Pa's business is here, and so many of our friends live here. This place will always be home to me."

It's harder for Ma than it is for me, Kelly thought. She just hides her feelings better, that's all. Kelly wanted desperately to say something comforting. "We will come back in the summer," she offered as consolation.

"I know, dear," Ma said, picking up the cups and carrying them into the kitchen. "We have that to look forward to, don't we?"

Kelly followed Ma into the kitchen. "It doesn't matter what happens," she said, hugging Ma, "as long as we are all together—you and Pa and Tim and me."

"That's right, Kelly," Ma said kissing her on the forehead. "Someday we will look back and think this was the best thing that ever happened to us."

It will take a long time before I can think that, but I'll trust Ma is right, Kelly thought.

That night in the quiet of her room with the lingering white light of late evening stealing through the bare window, Kelly looked at her gold one more time. She spread the nuggets on her sheet. There was just enough gold to carry out her plan.

When they got to Fairbanks, the first thing Kelly would do was ask a jeweler to make a watch chain of nuggets for Pa and a necklace for Ma. Pa wouldn't have to wear his watch on a plain chain anymore. No sir, he would have a chain studded with nuggets, like all the miners. Kelly would see to that.

They would walk down the street, Kelly and Pa, and he would show off his nugget chain saying, "Yes, sir, my daughter gave that to me. She worked all summer mining the gold."

Kelly whispered into her pillow, "It was worth it, Pa. It was worth every minute of it."

The Author and Illustrator

Kelly's story, *Gold City Girl*, could only have been written by someone who like Kelly grew up in Alaska and loved it.

For Jo Anne Wold, home has always meant Alaska, and she lives today in Fairbanks, the state's second largest city. She has done newspaper writing and recently published a collection of historical sketches, *Fairbanks, The $200 Million Gold Rush Town*, illustrated with historical photographs.

Because pioneering days in Alaska are comparatively recent (Fairbanks was incorporated in 1903), Miss Wold as a child had many opportunities to hear stories of early settlers. She visited the creek towns and learned the tales of the gold rush days. Her writing reflects not just this exciting part of Alaskan life, however, for the beauty of the natural world is very much present in her work.

George Armstrong, who illustrated Kelly's story, lives in Wilmette, Illinois. In addition to being an artist and mapmaker, Mr. Armstrong is a folk singer, bagpiper, and co-author with his wife Gerry of three colorful picture books, *The Magic Bagpipe*, *The Boat on the Hill*, and *The Fairy Thorn*. The authentic detail in Mr. Armstrong's pictures comes from careful research and the feel that he has for the American past.